In Late Summer

MAGDALENA BLAŽEVIĆ

*Translated from the Croatian
by Anđelka Raguž*

Linden Editions

Linden Editions, 110 Standen Rd, London SW18 5TS
www.lindeneditions.com

This English language edition published in the UK in 2025 by Linden Editions
First published by Fraktura, Zagreb, Croatia in 2022 with the title *U kasno ljeto*

Copyright © Magdalena Blažević 2022
English translation copyright © Anđelka Raguž 2025

The moral rights of the author have been asserted. The right of Magdalena Blažević to be identified as the author of this work has been asserted in accordance with Section 77 of the Copyright, Designs and Patents Act 1988.

All rights reserved. No part of this publication may be reproduced or transmitted in any form or by any means, electronic or mechanical, including photocopy, recording, or any information storage and retrieval system, without permission in writing from the publisher.

Quotation on p. 7 from *The Sound and the Fury* reproduced with the permission of Curtis Brown Group Ltd, London, on behalf of the estate of William Faulkner. Copyright © William Faulkner. Quotation on p. 7 from 'Fate Playing' reproduced with the permission of the estate of Ted Hughes and Faber and Faber Ltd. Copyright © Ted Hughes.

9 8 7 6 5 4 3 2 1

ISBN: 978-1-0687404-2-8
eISBN: 978-1-0687404-3-5

A CIP catalogue record for this book is available from the British Library

Cover image © Maria Nurek
Cover design © Tasja Puławska
Text design and typesetting by Tetragon, London
Printed in England by CMP (UK) Ltd.

This book was published with the financial support of the
Ministry of Culture and Media of the Republic of Croatia

Republic
of Croatia
Ministry
of Culture
and Media
Republika
Hrvatska
Ministarstvo
kulture
i medija

*To the residents of Kiseljak,
in memory of 16 August 1993*

Some days in late August at home are like this, the air thin and eager like this, with something in it sad and nostalgic and familiar.

WILLIAM FAULKNER,
The Sound and the Fury

>Like the first thunder cloudburst engulfing
>The drought in August
>When the whole cracked earth seems to quake
>And every leaf trembles
>And everything holds up its arms weeping.

TED HUGHES,
'Fate Playing'

I

CREAKS AND RATTLES

Look! This is my doll Julija and me. We're lying on the fold-out sofa in the living room because I still don't have my own room. In the evening, Mother takes the bed linen out of the drawer underneath the sofa. Click-clack. The bedsheet flies through the air like thinly stretched-out dough, and I stand on the wooden armrest, waiting to throw myself into the emptiness. It looks like a heap of feathers from Mother's pillow. Before the sun rises, I crawl into Mother and Father's bed, which is still warm from their bodies. I always lie on Mother's side, because I like how it smells of the blue scarf often attached to the mirror's frame. Roses and sweetened boiled milk. The hole is small at first, like my index finger, and then gets bigger and bigger. The feathers are dry, squeaky snow from the field. The softness only lasts a moment. Mother's slap is the ice beneath the dry snow, the hard sofa under the sheet. My skin burns for a long time. Father brought Julija home from a trip. He drives a lorry and that's why he's never home. He comes home at night when Mother has grown tired of waiting and watching through the window. Julija and I have big blue eyes. I've just taken her out of the box and her hair smells of fruit sweets. Father bought those too. The wrappers rustle beneath my fingertips, the sweets are sweet and sour. I feel sorry that Julija can't try any.

'Don't eat hard-boiled sweets lying down,' my mother warns.

Too late, it's slipped and become stuck in my throat.

I'm seven and going to school in the autumn. They've already bought me a school bag. My father grabs me by the legs, lifts me up high and starts shaking me roughly. It doesn't help. He lies me down on the sofa and starts hitting me on the back. Mother's voice is ever softer. Darkness drops over my eyes. I've stopped breathing.

This isn't the end. It can't be. I've got another seven years of life ahead of me. My father forces his fingers down my throat and pulls out the cherry-flavoured sweet. I cough for a long time, my throat hurting from Father's fingers and my back from his slaps. Why's Mother crying? I'm alive!

I'm standing here after so many years. The floury dirt from the driveway sticks to my bare, bloodied feet. The air is still just as hot. It blurs my eyesight, makes me dizzy.

Do you have anything to hold on to?

I can't remember where I lost my shoes. Did I leave them on the concrete slab under the window, upstairs in our house, or did they slip off on the staircase?

Can you hear the wood creaking?

Not beneath my body. No! I'm as light as a chick. It creaks under the firmly tightened black boots. Only Death wears such boots. Oh, how his body rattles!

I'll push my fingers into my ears and pull out the creaking and rattling.

∗

No one cares about Julija any more. She's lying in the dark in a wooden toy chest under the bed in my room, her eyes open wide, stuck.

Mother's just got back home from the hospital. She's still on crutches, and it takes her a while to climb the stairs up to my room in the attic. She drops the crutches in front of the door and grabs the doorknob with a shaky hand. She stands there staring through the frosted glass pane in the door. My desk, lamp and old typewriter can be made out through it. The smell of blinds and the dusty green carpet inside. Father had cut it to fit the room and cover the concrete. Mother's right leg drags behind her as if it belongs to someone else. She limps to my bed, lies down and buries her head in the pillow. She thinks she's going to find my scent there, but all she finds is the heat of her own breath and salt from her eyes. Crying is exhausting; Mother falls asleep. Her restless eyelids make it clear that her dream is troubled. The setting sun fills the room with a dark yellow light. It's the most beautiful light on a summer's day. Mother wakes up and sees the dust motes vibrating in the air. Slowly and lethargically, like the cooing of the doves under the roof. She drops to the floor, dragging her leg like a baby who hasn't learnt to crawl yet. She combs the carpet, looking for a blond hair or even an eyelash. She finds nothing, just old dirt and crumbs. Out of the desk drawer, she takes a sheet of paper with typed poems, hairpins, imitation jewellery, small, unusually shaped rocks, and shards of glass in various colours with smooth edges. Out of the wardrobe, she takes a black suitcase, whose buckles have fallen off, a diary and Julija. She puts them in the wooden toy chest and pushes it under the bed.

If you opened it, you would discover that Julija's hair still smells of fruit sweets.

The clock will soon strike five. The sun is a large ripe apple. It scorches and strikes the back of the head. The clear sky is heavy, pressing onto my shoulders and pushing my body into the ground. My legs shake, my knees give way.

I can't hide from Death.

There's a hedge of blue spruce behind me, its needles ravens' claws, hungry, pointy beaks. They easily pierce the thin fabric of my white dress made from old bedsheets. They were part of Mother's dowry. Before me is Grandmother's badly disfigured apple tree, its branches cut back to the trunk. It hasn't borne fruit for years; it's just waiting for someone to cut it down. It can't carry on like this, without a shadow and flowers. All that remains of the bench under the apple tree is a rotting skeleton. Death leans against it, his foot resting on the bench.

Have a good look at him!

Death has a gentle face, his eyes not visible beneath the cocked cap. It's soft and dark green like forest moss. We are separated by a low barbed-wire fence, along which grow roses with drooping, faded heads. A gentle breeze could blow them away. The fence was put up by Grandfather. He always carries an axe and hammer with him; he sharpens stakes and drives them deep into the ground. He never leaves a job unfinished.

The forest beckons. It roars like the river, like the train. The black conifers smell inviting. When alight, they pound like a torrent on a tin roof. Hail. New Year's fireworks.

Men's bodies are unstoppable rock avalanches.

Can you hear them forging their way towards the village?

Soon, they'll descend through dried-up streams and forest trails into our yard, spread out through the village like maggots.

Don't waste time trying to hide!

The tip of the green rock still protrudes from the dirt on the road. The grassy strip in the middle of the road goes all the way to the swamp. Blue chicory flowers grow on it. Their eyes open. Mother picks them.

'They're her eyes,' she thinks. 'They shouldn't be strewn along the road. More and more of them. What will I do with them? What?'

The door to Grandmother's cellar stands wide open, just like she used to keep it in summer, letting the hot air penetrate and slightly warm the thick, cold walls. The door has dried up and hangs there, stuck in the concrete like an ingrown nail. The semi-darkness smells of sprouting potatoes and rot, of motionless dust. There's no more sofa or table, just the wooden display cabinet. The glass panes have fallen out of the top half, but the coloured paper that Grandmother placed under the coffee cups and gold-decorated glasses is still there. The cupboard with the key can't be closed any more; the humidity has swollen the wood. Grandmother used to keep coffee, the coffee grinder and sugar cubes in it. When she unlocked it, the cellar would smell wonderful for a moment. Later, Grandfather hid his rakija in it. Plastic chairs, toolboxes and things that nobody needs any more are all lined up against the wall. A picture of the Virgin Mary still hangs on the wall by the door. Her head bowed, covered with a blue stole, her eyes sad. The Virgin Mary must have sad eyes. Her heart is as big as the sun, like a ripe apple. It takes up half the picture. It'll be pierced by seven swords.

The windows in the cellar are low, fixed to the road, and you can't see the sky or the forest through them, just the road and the feet of passers-by. I recognise Mother's. She walks slowly, the hem of her flowery dress swinging to and fro. You can push a finger into the scars on her leg. A bucket of overripe tomatoes sways in her hand. Clods of damp earth fall off her rubber galoshes. They disappear behind our house. I put my hands on the cold pane.

My name is Ivana. I lived for fourteen summers, and this is the story of my last.

II

SAINT JOHN'S EVE

Clear your head in the morning air! Even in summer, the mornings are fresh and blue here. The fog surrenders quickly; the sun disperses it like a dream. Can you smell the old hay? My brother's taken it out of the barn. He's already been in the forest. There are dry hazel and hornbeam branches in Grandmother's yard. He's naked to the waist, scratched all over and sweaty, covered in dust from the haystack. He strips with the first rays of the summer sun, like Father when he works around the house, and doesn't dress until the first autumn showers. Tonight, we're going to light a bonfire in the centre of the dirt track midway between Grandmother's house and ours. My cousin Dunja and I stand next to one another, waiting for the fire to catch and spring to life, to scorch our cheeks. We tie our hair into a knot at the top of our heads so that it doesn't catch like hay. We run up from the top of the dirt track and leap over the fire, higher than the rooftops. We flicker in the boiling-hot air and go out in the dust. That's how fireflies light up and go out in the dark of night. If you catch them and press them to your skin, they leave a shiny trail. They can't fly after and fall into the grass, flickering slowly for a long time until they go out completely. My brother leaps last. None of the children in the villages can jump as high as he can; he could be an athlete if he trained. He's not much older than me, but he's much taller. Mother says that boys grow like reeds in water. Thin bulrushes.

Mother sends me to the spring for mineral water every day, because she doesn't like leaving the house. She can see everything, anyway, from the window that looks out onto the road and the houses below the forest. In winter and summer, they're all covered by a cold, damp shadow. We've got it much better below the road, where it's flat and sunny. We are separated from the open field and river by the swamp and train tracks. I go everywhere by bike. I inherited the bike from my brother because it was already a dinosaur then, and now, while I'm bumping across the potholed asphalt, it seems like it's going to fall apart. Among crumpled newspapers in the basket behind me, empty bottles of rakija clink. Grandmother gathers them from around the shed and Grandfather's workshop and puts them away under the stairs next to the cellar door. She never finds any bottle tops. Once Grandfather has opened a bottle, he doesn't need the top any more. The open necks stink even after we've washed them with sand and well water.

I turn off the road towards the spring. The fountains of mineral water are snowy, alive. Mother says that my hair's the same: a white, untameable waterfall. I don't let her comb and braid my hair any more. I like it down, bouncing when I run. The spring was once surrounded by a high metal fence with pointy tips, thin arrows looking up into the sky. They looked like shouldered rifles. My brother always carries an air rifle. He takes shots at birds and empty bottles. Mother's afraid he'll blind us with it; she yells after him, warns him, but he runs off into the fields. He says he's as accurate as a soldier and that she need not worry. There's no fence around the spring now, and you can touch the fountains. On the concrete frame is a build-up of rust-coloured residue, as soft as freshly squeezed-out paint. A thin pipe protrudes from the concrete frame. Mineral water spurts from it like blood from a just-cut chicken neck. I fill the bottles with bubbles. Everyone knows the water's healthy and that it's better for dough than yeast, so Mother makes our bread with it. In the village, they drink mineral water instead of still water, which I can't understand because it's flavourless and makes me want to vomit.

I place the wet bottles into the basket. I push sheets of newspaper between them. The mineral water makes the faded letters and pictures go dark. Nothing grows around the spring; the ground, trodden bare and rusty, stinks of sulphur and iron. Green algae cling to flavourless little puddles.

The forest is above the spring, its edge guarded by wild chestnuts, shiny branched giants with sharp serrated leaves. Dunja says that the treetops are full of squirrel nests, and that sometimes baby squirrels fall out of the nests onto the grass. They remind me of newborn piglets, pink and hairy, except they're completely blind. Grandmother's sow went dry once. Grandfather heaped the piglets into the wheelbarrow and emptied them into the hole by the train tracks; that's where we throw everything that dies. He was followed to the train tracks by ravens and blowflies. The sow was left lying in the corner of the sty with red swollen teats.

Gnarled witches' fingers slid the roots of the chestnut under the wide concrete stairs that lead to the village tavern on the hill and tilted them. The tavern is a low white building with a flat roof, broken windows and torn, blackened curtains. Clumps of grass grow in the cracks in the concrete patio, choked by red dodders. There are no more chairs or parasols on the terrace. Toppled beer bottles and trodden-on cigarette butts lie strewn along the length of the wall. The terrace used to be full of people; men would relax there after work before going home late in the evening. Our grandfather never drank in the tavern.

The bike pedal squeaks. The muddy wheels turn lethargically and then pick up speed. The wind hits me in the face and lifts my hair.

A flying white, silky flag.

IN THE MIDDLE
OF THE NIGHT

If you look around you, you'll see that the village was deserted a long time ago. Gates padlocked on both sides of the road. Ivy and tiny rose vines have made their way around the iron railings. The hissing of vipers and adders, and green lizards among the lush weeds in the gardens, sunbaking on the concrete along the houses as if on a hot pebbly beach. Disintegrating ribbons for tying up plants hang from stakes in the gardens. On patios, tables with nailed-down plastic tablecloths are covered in smooth black ink, and buried under leaves and twigs.

Drip, drip, drip, drip...
The roofs of the abandoned houses drip, caved in by rain and snow. The drops drum, tap until the roof tiles move apart; bird nests in the cracks.

Can you hear the chirping of open beaks in the rotting drainpipes?

Worms wriggling in their throats. If they don't strengthen their bare wings before the rains, the torrent will take them directly into the cat's mouth. The wild tomcat, larger than all the other tomcats, makes the rounds of the houses. He sniffs and spits, eats birds and kittens. He kills them before they can even open their eyes.

Drip, drip, drip, drip...
    Walls swell. Fungi sprout from poison moss in dark corners; they crumble at the touch. These are little white lilies from our garden. Mother puts them down under the wooden cross; their fragrance diffuses into the golden dust.

We didn't see anyone with suitcases, because that's how you flee in the middle of the night. Dawn found windows covered with green fabric and brown blankets with tigers, instead of curtains. Even though the abandoned houses were locked, life in them was just beginning: they were conquered by companies of ants and termites, long-legged spiders set traps, mice emerged from floors. English ivy crept behind façades and through dried-up window frames.

Spasoje stayed behind. He would never abandon his house. It's the oldest in the village and he's been living in it alone for a long time. The window shutters, handmade from old boards, are open. While his father was alive, the house served as a store. It used to be full of grain, wheat and sauerkraut. The shelves were filled with jars from yellow to black. You could take goods home and pay later by pawning a piece of land. He had so many fields that he never got around to all of them. Spasoje only leaves the house to go to the village field, and to the church in town twice a year. At Christmas and Easter.

The roof tiles have gone black, covered in places by thick moss. Apple tree branches have fallen on them. Apples at our fingertips, but we don't pick them. Dunja says that the house is haunted, and that thumps and cries can be heard at night. I don't believe this, but I'm afraid of Spasoje. When the playground is very noisy, he comes out into the street with an axe and yells. Dunja says he must be possessed, and then we go home through the forest.

He's sitting on the wooden veranda, tiny and hunched over, in the dust, among dirty old bottles and scattered leather shoes. He wears his fur hat in winter and summer. His hair is grey and messy, his eyes tiny, barely noticeable in his crinkled skin. Splinters fly all around him from under the axe on the old tree stump. My feet hurry of their own accord when I pass his house, my heart pounds manically. I only stop at the fence if I see him heading towards the fields with a basket on his back. His fields are full of self-seeding crab apples good for vinegar and runny black apple sauce, which Grandmother pours over cooked pumpkin just before Christmas. The hay barn is always bolted; hay pokes out between the boards all the way to the roof. They say that there's a cow in there so big that she can't get through the door, but I've never heard mooing. Spasoje never married. The village says he had an ill-fated love affair, but Grandmother thinks that it's because he is miserly. The houses in the village haven't had numbers for a long time; a completely rusted plate with the number eight is all that remains on his door.

On both sides of the road there are tall alders; the tops of their canopies form a tunnel. The sun doesn't penetrate them, so the leaves of the large elder are dark green in the shade.

The tunnel smells of dusty yellow flowers and cold spring water.

Drip, drip, drip, drip...

FOOL

It's the middle of the night, but desire is keeping Spasoje's eyes wide open. In the cold darkness he is overcome by heat, thinking about the black hair that peeks out from beneath Budimka's headscarf; her skin is white and smooth, like milk that has just gone sour. Tomorrow he'll put on his old-fashioned black trousers, an ironed white shirt, his waistcoat trimmed with red thread and a woollen coat. It's still ten days to Lent, enough time for Budimka to come down off the mountain and into his home. It'll be nice for her here; it's always icy and cold up there. They'll work together in the fields during the day, and at night... Spasoje thinks of the smell of basil and hay at her breast, the thin waist under her dress. He rubs his burning face with his hands. He rehearses what he's going to say when he stands before her. She'll smile at him just like she does when she goes home from the fields.

He doesn't need more than half an hour to walk to Budimka's. Down the muddy path and then uphill, through the orchard and the forest. Don't say a thing to anyone! It can't wait any more; it must happen before Lent. Easter is an eternity away; he won't make it. The ground is patchy beneath the forest canopy, the odd orchis peeking out from under the snow. His heart pounds because of the steep slope, from desire and fear. Another moment and he'll be standing in front of her house.

Budimka sees him from the window.
'Fool!'
She comes down the steps and throws a woollen shawl over her shoulders. She takes her embroidery and sits down on the veranda as if she's been sitting like that all morning. Spasoje feels as if the Virgin Mary herself has appeared to him. His voice trembles, his words formal, as if he's speaking from the pulpit. They must get married immediately; there's no reason to wait.

Budimka laughs out loud and lifts her gaze from her embroidery.
It seems to Spasoje that the sun has risen somewhere and lit up his face. He can't see clearly. He rubs his eyes with his sleeve, in vain.
'What's the rush, Spaso? Come back after Easter when the weather has thawed, and we'll see then.'
Budimka seems distant and odd to Spasoje. Her laughter echoes in his head.
He flies down the hill. His feet never touch the ground. It isn't a downward slope any more, but an abyss.
'Fool! Fool!'

A BONE

Our dirt track turns off the road between two winged pine trees. They cast a shadow over Grandmother's house, which is small, white and pink. Grandmother and Grandfather moved from the first floor into the cellar recently, because it's dug deep into the ground and serves as our shelter. Grandfather has protected the windows with sandbags and logs. The already dark cellar has sunk into complete darkness and transformed into a mouse hole. Grandmother can't see the old apple tree, the table and bench, or the thin lilac branches and their purple flowers from the window looking out onto the road and forest.

Can you feel how full of cold they are?

Not even the sun can chase it away. I cram picked flowers into my pockets. There, in the darkness, they wither and dry out immediately. Their fragrance lingers. The fruit of the old apple tree are still tiny and hard, dark green. Dunja and I can't wait for the apples to ripen. When Grandmother isn't looking, we beat them with poles. They fall to the ground and where they collide with the ground, they soften. Grandmother says we can't eat green apples, that we'll get mouse fever and die. We wonder what this scary disease is like, but we've never been sick. Our teeth can barely penetrate the hard flesh; the sour juice makes our mouths contract. When he planted the apple tree, Grandfather made a table and bench for it. Tiny bugs fall onto the table from the canopy and stick to the emptied coffee cups. There's an ants' nest in the sugar bowl. A grapevine winds itself around the apple tree. That's why Grandmother doesn't let us climb it. The grape clusters are tiny, like withered lilac flowers.

Our house is big; wooden stairs lead to the top floor, which is unused and empty because Father intends it for my brother when he gets married. It's all concrete and large windows. On the stairs, you can already smell the minute, sharp dust. Mother has stuck curtains on the windows so that the house looks prettier from the road. They're black, rigid and dusty. Camomile flowers are drying by the wall, on a table covered with a clean tablecloth.

You have to be quiet here; voices echo in an empty room like on leafless forest heights. Upstairs in the attic, doves coo and flap their wings from dawn onwards. When night comes or rain pours down, they fall silent.

The bike squeaks and slows down, turns onto the road between the two pine trees and speeds down the gentle slope. The wheel catches on the tip of a green rock and hops. A floury yellow cloud rises around me. Glass shatters, scattering tiny bubbles onto the dust. A deep gash on my knee; the bone is as white as my hair.

My brother's calling me. I show him my knee.

'That's nothing,' he says.

He picks me up and carries me into the house. He smells of sweat and hay, of dusty heat.

We leave a red trail behind us along the silver ash fence. The wheels of the broken bike turn slowly amid the smashed bottles. The bubbles find their way through the dust and soak into the ground. I look at the sky. In the middle of the clear sky, a flock of magpies soars and plunges, a black show.

The air thunders. The forest darkens.

THE SMALL SUITCASE

The double bed rises like a dumper. Mother sleeps turned towards the window, the embroidered net curtains and thick green blackout curtains. I see her opening them in the morning. She drapes the bed covers and fluffed pillows over the windowsill to air out. Small goose feathers and slow dust motes fall out of them. Her nightgown open at her large, saggy breasts, her sleeves rolled up. Mother's skin is dark, but thin and translucent, as smooth as a bat's wing. Her eyes are green glass, bottles full of bubbles. From the window, their gaze falls on the well lid with the iron handle, on the tap with the old water hose coiled around it and on the thin pear tree whose fruit are hard until winter. No birds or bees dare to land on it.

Under the bed, the scent of yellowing pressed linen and coats; the sachets of dry flowers have lost their perfume. Under the coats is a small black fake-leather suitcase with wonky silver buckles. A small accordion drops out of it and hits the floor with a drawn-out dissonance. Nobody knows how to play it. Inside, the suitcase is lined with golden-yellow cardboard.

'Don't overfill your suitcases; we'll be back soon,' Mother says.

I pack two pairs of shorts, a dress, some T-shirts, a notebook, pencils and a toothbrush into the small suitcase. Sivka wraps herself around my legs and meows. I let her into the house even though Grandmother says that a cat's place isn't in the house, and that you can die if you swallow a cat hair.

I'm separated from Dunja's house by a large vegetable and flower garden. It's edged with chrysanthemums and sunflowers. The sunflower stalks are needle-like, the leaves hairy, still green, and beanstalks coil around them in the same way that the ivy wraps itself around the trees along the riverbank. The flower bed is soft from all the digging and watering, which is why Mother goes into the garden in rubber galoshes. Later, she puts them, heavy with mud, on the grass by the tap. Grandfather also planted a domestic variety of apple tree on the slope above Dunja's house. The fruit are large and green. Round children's heads. They fall from a great height and crack on the ground. The cracked flesh rots quickly. Dunja says that at night small rodents visit the garden and feast on the fruit. That's why there are deep holes in the fallen apples. The tree outgrew the house a long time ago and casts its shadow over the skylight. The skylight is full of stars when the night skies are clear, and then there's no point reading. The shelf next to Dunja's bed is crowded with books, some of which we took from the school library. The roof had fallen in, and bundles of books were lying scattered on the floor. We picked up two bundles: that was all we could carry. Dunja said it wasn't stealing, because the books would have been destroyed by mould as soon as it rained.

Dunja kneels in front of her billy goat, Bekan, who is tied to a stake. Camomile blooms in the field in front of the house. She sees me and jumps up.

'Bekan and Sivka have to come with us!'

She's afraid that Grandfather will forget to feed them, and animals can go crazy from hunger.

Aunt and Dunja have already packed their bags.

The air has stilled, like it does in winter when the temperature drops below zero. The silence is cut at times by the mooing of cows and the squealing of pigs that refuse to be forced out of their barns and sties to be slaughtered. Sivka waits for me on the doorstep. My leg hurts and I walk slowly because of the tight bandage around my knee. I open the door and let her into the house. I take tiny walnuts out of a hamper and scatter them around the pantry, and I put Sivka inside. I fasten the lid with a piece of old wire. Mother looks at me reproachfully but says nothing; she just dismisses me with a wave of her hand. We barely have time to buckle up the suitcases, my brother is already carrying them out front. Grandmother is already sitting on the well lid and tightening the knot on her headscarf behind her head. Tears stream around her nose towards her thin, pale lips, into her toothless mouth. Grandfather comes out of the cellar and puts her suitcase on the grass.

THE KNOT ON THE HEADSCARF

Grandmother is fleeing from the axe, barefoot, and runs onto the road. In her nightgown. She's holding her head.

'What will I do without my headscarf?'

She's as bald as a newborn baby.

My father grabs the axe from Grandfather, who is yelling louder than cornered wild game. My father is yelling too, but his voice is lost in Grandfather's yelling. When he goes berserk, nobody can overpower him. He disappears into the darkness. Grandmother ties her headscarf in the cellar and turns the key twice in the lock. She manages to fall asleep just before dawn, when exhaustion has overridden her fear. She awakens to the sound of the phone ringing. She keeps it on a stool near the sofa; they've just had it installed and she's still not used to its cutting ringtone. The phone seems to be bouncing up and down. She tightens the knot on the headscarf; she knows that the call is from the village, about Grandfather. They've found him in a stream or ditch. My father and uncle go to get him; they load him into the car or wheelbarrow and unload him onto the sofa in the cellar. Grandfather lies on the sofa as still as a corpse. Dunja and I raise his eyelids – cloudy, bloodshot eyes beneath them. They have none of their usual sparkle. Grandmother chases us away: this is not for children. Father turns the shed and workshop upside down. He empties everything he finds in bottles. He never drinks: lorry drivers must always be sober.

'When he doesn't drink, he's as good as gold.'
As she speaks, Grandmother's hands reach for the knot on her headscarf.

I can't remember Grandmother ever having hair. Dunja says she must have been born old. Her hair started falling out as soon as Grandfather brought her to his house.

She's seventeen and she sleeps with her head covered. The house is at the foot of the mountain, covered by the forest's shadow which is as black as tar. The calls of the night birds sound as if someone is tapping on the windowpanes, crying and pulling at the iron bolt on the door. The forest only falls silent in the morning, when mice start squeaking in the mousetraps. She's glad that they all sleep in the same room. Before dawn, green stains emerge on the walls and ceiling, and in Grandmother's imagination every stain has a mouth and claws.

Grandfather left Grandmother in the house at the foot of the mountain and went into the navy for three years. He only came home on short leave, and Grandmother gave birth every year like a fertile and fruitful field. Her thighs expanded; she found pieces of her teeth in mouthfuls of bread. In the mornings, she gathered strands of hair from the pillowcase.
She cries in front of the wedding photograph.

*

She's standing beside Grandfather in the photo studio; they're to be married in a couple of days. Ducats borrowed from the village jingle around her neck; a white blouse rustles under her fingertips. Grandfather's shirt is cut low on the chest and singed, with sharp blades of grass poking out. He's a lot taller than her. It seems to her that the top of his head is a canopy, and that it's breaking through the ceiling. Grandmother doesn't lift her gaze. Green eyes prey on her from beneath steep awnings; a wide jaw and shiny, sharp teeth threaten.

The photograph is small, black-and-white. They're taking it to be painted on larger paper; it's to be Grandmother and Grandfather's wedding portrait. It hangs on the wall above the bed in the upstairs bedroom. Grandmother looks at it for a long time: they've been painted from the waist up, the couple's heads are on a level. She's in a lace wedding dress, a thin veil over her head, translucent and as light as a breath of air, framing her brown curls. Her ears are adorned with earrings; a pearl necklace with a locket hangs around her neck. Grandmother can feel how gentle and cool they are. She's holding a bouquet of white roses, both buds and in full bloom. She can't recognise any of her own lines in the portrait; only the eyes are hers, the eyebrows furrowed at the root, her gaze into the distance. Grandmother wonders what it would be like to be the girl in the wedding portrait. The young man in the tie is a fitting match for her. The rosemary on his lapel smells of the garden; his hair is neatly combed back and he has soft boyish features. Such eyes don't flash like lightning, don't cloud before nightfall. They remind Grandmother of the eyes of saints in paintings.

The young man's arms are gentle and hug her waist.

Big babies drop out of Grandmother; they grow like reeds in the water. Grandmother looks into their eyes, turning them towards the sun. She's afraid that they will flash green.

They're all as dark as night. Grandmother kisses and kisses them.

THE BEAR'S PAW

It's dawn and Grandfather's shouting. A pheasant feather inserted in his hat, as straight as an arrow, and he has a carbine on his shoulder. He's the best hunter in the village. Grandmother is walking around, putting bread, bacon, onion and rakija into his bags. In front of the house, drooling muzzles bark, as piercing as men's throats. They only quieten down in the forest when they sense the prey. Grandfather's green eye focuses, his hands are calm. He never pulls the trigger in vain.

Grandmother doesn't go back to bed. She throws her barn coat over her shoulders and picks up the tin pail. She's used to the morning darkness, the frost and the damp. The pail hits the concrete, and Betsy's tail whips her across the face like a sharp corn leaf. The pigs get up out of their filth and start squealing. Grandmother curses the pigs and Betsy, until the sound of milk hitting the tin pail calms her.

Grandmother pours the milk into a large round pan and puts it on the stove to boil. Later, a fatty cream forms. She eats it with jam and coffee while a stag looks down at her from the wall. Its antlers are cold, rough crowns and its eyes are black marbles, clouded by dust just like Grandfather's are when he falls into a ditch. Grandmother wipes them with a wet rag and they come to life for a moment. Dunja's pockets and mine are full of marbles. They clink as we run, they roll on the ground and stop in dirt holes. We don't have any black ones; all of ours are clear glass. We turn them towards the sun. Green eyes look at us from within.

Even foxes have marbles instead of eyes. Just smaller ones. They don't hang on walls, but bite their own tails curled around female necks. They're orange or grey-white. Their fur is first snowflake-like and soft, but it moults quickly, and then firm, white skin peeps out from beneath. Our grandmother never wears a fox around her neck. In winter, she's in her loose black coat, and on her head she wears a woollen headscarf sprinkled with dry flowers, from light yellow to dark red. When in mourning, Grandmother wears a black headscarf.

Grandfather's dogs, miniature dachshunds, were poisoned one winter. If he ever finds out who did it, he will break both their legs. While he's shouting, he raises his bear's paw – that's what Grandmother calls Grandfather's right hand. It's big and covers her whole face. A hunting rifle exploded in his hand once, but he didn't let them take him to hospital, so the hand healed by itself; the tips of his fingers remain stiff and bent. Grandfather's bear's paw is no hindrance; it serves as a tool. Grandmother's skin remembers it well. It's dry and rough, like the dusty potatoes from the cellar. A large mousetrap, squeaky and rusty. You can't escape its grasp.

BITTER ALMONDS

We descend to the country road through the swamp and over the train tracks; only tractors use the railway crossing. Water splashes and squelches under our feet because the swamp is also damp in summer, full of fish pools bordered by reeds and bulrushes. There are frogs and tadpoles in them and fatty carp on the muddy bottom. After school, Dunja and I are in the swamp, wearing rubber boots. Dunja is carrying a plastic basin for the turtles, and she keeps them in it till the evening. She then brings them back to where she found them, because she's afraid they'll be dead by morning. She catches turtles and frogs with her bare hands. Grandmother tells her that frogs pissed on her hands once, and that's why she has so many warts on them. Grandmother sends her to pick fleawort at new moon and tells her to rub her warts with it. She sits on the grass and murmurs, looking up at the sky:

> Moon, Moon!
> Now so new
> Remove these lumps
> From me soon.

Later, the warts dry up and drop off.

✼

Grandmother and Aunt yell at Dunja because she's lagging behind. Bekan refuses to move, digging his hooves into the ground, bleating loudly. Dunja is dragging him along by the rope, pulling with all her might. The basket in my hand swings like the steelyard balance when they weigh us. Sivka can't settle. My knee's hurting, the bandage seeping, but I'm hurrying as fast as I can.

I never look into the gaps along the railway line. I'm afraid that I'll be sucked in. This is where Grandmother's Betsy ended up. She died after they pulled a stillborn calf out of her. She had spent the whole day mooing and bellowing, so Grandfather tied one end of a long rope to the calf's legs sticking out of Betsy and the other to our red Lada. Father turned on the ignition and put the car into gear, while Grandfather and Uncle tugged as hard as they could. It was not clear who was screaming the loudest – Grandfather, Uncle, Betsy or the car. The calf fell out onto the hay, black and motionless. Grandfather loaded it onto the wheelbarrow like the piglets and unloaded it into the hole. Betsy lay down and died before dawn. Grandmother stood by the tap and cried while Grandfather cut Betsy into pieces with a large knife and axe. He made several trips to unload her into the hole. Grandmother threw the bloody hay onto the dung heap and scoured the concrete with buckets of water. It's different with cats. Grandfather waits till they've been weaned and then, in the early morning, he stuffs them into a sack with a large rock. Dunja and I don't cry, because the first kittens must always be thrown into the water. The Bosna is muddy and rapid; it takes everything it sinks far away and covers it with slimy water grass.

We cross the rusty tracks and descend to the country road. Pheasants scream in the hedges along the fields.

The road has transformed into a colourful procession, loud and dusty. We're going to a village across the Bosna where our great-aunt lives in a small house. We'll be safer there, far from our forest. Tractors loaded with old women and children make their way ahead of us. Cows are tied to trailers, followed by women with willow switches. Grandmother says the cows are more obedient than the children, and that's why they don't fight much, only when they're in heat.

Bekan appears to have calmed down, but Dunja is still holding on to the rope tightly. In the hamper, Sivka seems to have fallen asleep from exhaustion.

Along the fields, the blossoming hawthorn bushes smell of bitter almonds.

THE CHRISTMAS TREE

Ilonka and Karlo are walking side by side through the cornfield. The stalks are still green and thin, and broken now. Karlo outgrew Ilonka a long time ago; his head is a blooming sunflower on a thin stalk. His face bears the lines of our neighbour, Đuka.

'The devil take them!'
Đuka turns his head away from Ilonka and Karlo.

'He's mine! He hasn't got a father! And I... I'm as innocent as the Virgin Mary!' Ilonka repeatedly told the village.
She won't let go of him. Like a Gypsy, she carried him in a scarf until he couldn't fit into it any more, her dress unbuttoned beneath the scarf. Salty skin, sweet milk.
She didn't let him cry.

'The devil take them! It can't be!'

A small stream and paddock separate us from Ilonka's small house. We never cross them. Nor does Karlo. She doesn't let him stray from her side. They're together in the fields and forest.
'He's mine alone!'

*

We're in the same class. We gather on the road. We walk to school in single file because there is only a narrow footpath between the road and the deep ditches. Ilonka doesn't let Karlo go alone; she walks at the head of the file gripping his hand. While we're in class, she waits for him patiently in the schoolyard. She sits on the concrete, leaning against the school fence, her legs spread wide apart, peeling an apple with a small knife. Ribbons of apple peel fall on her leather shoes. We can see under her skirt. Black hairs, as sharp as pieces of wire, stick out from her yellowing old underwear. As dusk falls on the way home after the afternoon school shift, Ilonka tells of children whose mothers cursed them, and how the devil himself came to take them; of black-haired *moras* that strangle young men in their sleep. Dunja squeezes my hand.

'Ilonka must be a witch!'

Ilonka felt as if a sugar cube was melting in her mouth whenever she saw Đuka. She followed him, her legs hurrying of their own accord. Hurry! He'll be gone!

She would turn up uninvited and work alongside him in the fields and forest. In the evening she would wait at his gate until he returned from the village. In the morning she would tap at his windows.

Her belly grew. Her breasts swelled. She couldn't do up her dress any more.

The locked gate shook in her grip.

'Đuka! Đuka!'

He was at the door, shouting.

He picked up two rocks and threw them over the gate at Ilonka.

She picked them up and put them in her pocket.

The teacher said, 'Read.'

Karlo opened his book, and followed the words with his finger, but they were quicker than his tongue. All Fs in the mark book. Laughter rang around the classroom. Raindrops spilt from his eyes onto the book and melted the black ink. The words disappeared completely.

The teacher, like Grandfather, stank of rakija. It oozed from his suit, from his skin. He would punish us with lashes of the rod. His name was Mirko: two lashes on the hands, on both sides. When he lashed us, he would purse his lips together and his eyes would bulge. Our hands trembled from the lashes; the welts burned. I tried to take hold of my pencil; I swallowed my tears.

He would come to the village in a red Fiat. We fled from our yards then into the orchards and hid in the canopies. If he caught us at home, he would sit us in his lap. The stench then was unbearable.

Ilonka was sitting beside the road between two plum orchards. She was striking rock against rock. The sparks of a curse. Her voice was strange, her prayer rising above the treetops and disbanding flocks of birds. She could hear hooves and a wedding song. She struck harder, prayed louder. A gust of wind raised the dust off the road. The plum branches came to life. The first drops were big and heavy; they beat the rustling red wreaths around the horses' heads and made the colours run. Red drops ran down the white muzzles. A plum branch took hold of the bride's veil and lifted it high. Đuka stood up to catch it, but in vain. The heavens opened and the frightened horses cantered away.

Night fell and the rain stopped. The wind calmed down. Ilonka got up and went home, down the road, holding her big belly in her hands. A veil as thin as a breeze fluttered in the plum canopy above her head.

Ilonka was tired of taking Karlo to school.
'He has a headache. He can't go to school.'
The doctor wrote a note and stamped it.
'He's mine!'
Karlo's world shrank to his yard, the forest and fields. They dragged in logs, and shouted while sawing them. Ilonka chopped them up; he put them away in the shed. They washed at the tap in front of the house; she held his hand, he was naked and clumsy. A newborn calf. His small limp member swung to and fro. We looked away. Ilonka's voice was drowned out by Karlo's screaming and the pounding of jets of water on the concrete.

Karlo is carrying a backpack on his back, stretched plastic bags in his hands. Ilonka is carrying an old black suitcase in one hand, and a small plastic Christmas tree in the other, some forgotten silver ornaments shining on it.
'Who knows when we'll be back. We can't have Christmas without a Christmas tree.'

YOU'LL FALL THROUGH
AND BREAK YOUR NECK!

The autumn is chilly and I'm heading along the tracks towards the bridge with Grandmother. I'm still small, only reaching up to her waist. She's yelling at me the whole time, gripping my hand in hers, and nearly breaking all my bones. The sleepers are spaced far apart from one another, and they seem to be racing ahead of us. If we miss one, our feet will crumple on the sharp ballast. Grandmother's feet are as small as mine, but wider; she barely squeezed them into her leather shoes.

We're close to the bridge; the roar is ever louder, so Grandmother shouts louder. We think we can hear a train behind us. We must be quick over the bridge because there is nowhere for us to move aside. It would cut us in two like Grandfather split the pig in two on the spreader. We mustn't miss a sleeper, because there's no ballast between them – just emptiness and the muddy river below and its enticing, threatening eddies. Grandmother loses her voice on the bridge; she's panting louder than the train and the river.

'Look where you're going!'

I can't avert my gaze. The eddies will suck me down. My heart thumps; it'll burst like overripe tomatoes under black boots. My legs give way. I trip. Droplets strike my face, from the river or Grandmother's mouth. Grandmother crushes my bones in her hand.

'You'll fall through and break your neck!'

You don't have to be afraid of the bridge any more. Look. The spaces between the sleepers have been boarded up, and the sleepers and tracks have been covered with pebbles and sand. Cars drive over it now. Trains don't pass by here any more anyway.

Don't be afraid!
It's just roaring. It can't hurt you.

SHELLS

Sit down and rest in the old armchair on the riverbank! It's beautiful: yellow velvet, carved wooden armrests. Life thrives in it, breaking through the fabric and blossoming green. Take one of the beautiful teacups. Pink rose bouquets, gold trimming. Here, there's one still unchipped. The fire's just gone out, the smoke's still rising from the singed clothes. Flowery summer dresses, creased black trousers. Polished shoes, bows and high heels. I may even find a pair if I dig in the heap. What size are you?

We took everything from the abandoned and destroyed houses, as if we had been let loose in the old village school full of Caritas donations. You elbow your way and fight over things. You stuff what you can grab into a bag and later exchange things for something your own size. Last spring, Dunja and I found some checked trousers. She said they were dreadful and she had no idea why someone would wear clown trousers, let alone pay for them. Furniture, cutlery, clothes and shoes all get new owners and both the owners and the things start adapting to unfamiliar scents, shapes and touches. Mouldy bread and unwashed dishes with leftover pie fly out of other people's ovens. What can't be used is thrown along the bank. The Bosna has always been trimmed with piles of rubbish: some of it is taken by the river when it rises, some of it is incinerated. Its banks are as dirty, but the water has never been clearer.

Empty snail shells are stuck to dry bushes. They're seashells, Dunja says. This was all under water once. They are everywhere; you just have to look carefully. On humid days we spray ourselves with water from the garden hose in the yard. We attach it to the tap and let it fill with water and then leave it in the sun to warm up. When we open the nozzle, a warm jet of water spurts out. It lasts only for a few moments. We scream. A muddy pool forms under our feet. We sunbake in the paddock, on large beach towels. Dunja takes the large shells from the display cabinet with the crystal. We press them to our ears and cover our heads with our T-shirts. The shells remember the sound of the sea and the waves; you just need to let go.

You turn round in vain; the village isn't visible any more. Just the forest.

BONFIRE

If the scent of sugar and popcorn was wafting in the air, I'd think we were at a village fair. Stifling air, children screaming and dust. I could perhaps convince you of it too. If I spun in the middle of the field that has been trodden bare, my hair would transform into a merry-go-round, my hands would smell of strawberry syrup and lubricated chains. They would clang like plastic pearls hanging on a rope from the tent top. Is this glittery confetti falling on us?

If the narrow road in the village across the Bosna wasn't overcrowded with tractors, people and cattle, you would see how cracked and churned up it was. On rainy days, you stumble into knee-deep ditches. The gates to the front yards are open, and the people leave the road and spread out across the meadows to stand in front of the houses, in the shade of dense canopies. Our great-aunt's house is on the road. It has her face. Slow, teary eyes blink in the windows; it exhales sour breath through the door, and the three wooden steps under the front door are lazily drooping lips. On the steps are overturned buckets and dried-up leftovers for the cats. Since she's been living by herself, Great-Aunt lets them enter the house freely. I open Sivka's hamper, and she jumps out. She first looks round cautiously, then finds herself on the steps smelling old bread. Grandmother has stopped in her tracks, exhausted, cold and sweaty; I can only hear her panting. If she doesn't sit down soon, she may drop dead. My brother has been carrying her suitcase the whole way, because carrying herself is already more than an effort for Grandmother. We put the suitcases down in the kitchen; my brother has put the rifle in the corner behind the sofa and disappeared. It's been a while since he let Mother know he was going out, and that's why Mother is always at the window, even when she isn't expecting my father. Grandmother collapses onto a sofa covered in cat hair, and Mother takes our things to the bedroom. Great-Aunt only has one bedroom. It has a double bed against one wall with a velvet bedspread on it. Peacocks with their tails spread out, and magnificent cockerels and golden apples. There's a colourful rug on the floor, and an open wooden wardrobe by the other wall, with a man's coat and shirts still hanging in it on coat hangers. On the coat's shoulder pads is a thick layer of dust. There are dresses shaped by wide thighs and enormous breasts.

Here too, Dunja and I are separated by a garden. Great-Aunt's daughter-in-law invited them to stay with her. Bekan is tied to a low flowerbed fence. Aunt and Dunja will be sleeping there until we're allocated one of the empty houses in the village. Great-Aunt is frying fritters. The dough floats on the boiling lard, drops splatter. We eat them hot with a mug of soured milk. The table is next to the window. I can see my brother preparing a bonfire in the field beneath the tall mulberry trees with the boys from the village. I've never seen a larger one. There is a dark-skinned boy among them, he is as dark as a Gypsy. His name is Goran.

It'll be dark soon.

*

Great-Aunt's house is as sooty as a chimney from the flame of the oil lamp. The smoke is quick and black and sticks to the walls in greasy layers like that on pots and pans used on wood stoves. No one has candles any more, except prayer candles, and we keep them for the cemetery. Mother and Grandmother make them: they thread thin rope through yellow wax, which they stretch through the whole house and then roll into a ball. The house is warm then and smells of honey, so the bees stick to the windows and buzz loudly.

Dunja is at the door; we're going to jump over the bonfire. She has left Bekan in the shed; he'll be spending the night there, because the door can be padlocked. Someone might try to steal him and cook him on a spit. Sivka stays behind, asleep under the table. Dunja says that it may not be so bad when we get our own houses. You never know. We may get rooms with rugs and wardrobes. We may like it and it could be better than being at home. The bonfire under the mulberry trees is much larger than the one on our road. My brother and Goran have jumped over it several times. Dunja is hesitant, checking if her hair is tied tightly. My leg still hurts, the blood on the bandage has dried and turned black. You can't jump over such a fire, no matter how high you jump. Dunja pulls me by the arm.

'We'll jump together.'

I free myself from her grip.

'Jump by yourself!'

People applaud.

'What's wrong with you, Blondie? You scared?'

Blood rushes to my face. Goran laughs at me and jumps as high as my brother.

I run home.

Great-Aunt pulls an old quilt from the bottom of the wardrobe and spreads it on the floor. The stuffing is hard and lumpy, the fabric slippery and cold. Mother and I are going to sleep on it. We put a sheet and a pillow on top of the quilt. It's enough for the two of us. Great-Aunt and Grandmother can barely fit in the bed. It creaks under their heavy bodies. They look like two large breasts with withered heads instead of nipples under the bedspread.

Mother opens the window. Grandmother disapproves; she's afraid she'll catch cold. The shadows on the walls flicker, the flame of the oil lamp pops. Mother blows it out and the shadows disappear.

She lies down next to me. She is motionless, but I can tell she's awake by her breathing. My brother's on the sofa in the kitchen. Sivka's in her hamper under the table. The musty stench of the pigsty drifts through the window. It mixes with the smell of dust and the stench of long-dried urine behind the door, which emanates from the large underwear that has dried yellow. Great-Aunt, like Grandmother, pees her pants when she coughs or laughs wholeheartedly. She, too, was like a fertile field. Grandmother boils her underwear in a large laundry pot, in water mixed with white powder. Soapsuds bubble on the surface, tiny pink balloons. Scorching white smoke emanates from the pot. Poisonous drops run down the walls and windows. I breathe into my hand.

*

'What's wrong with you, Blondie? You scared?'

Goran's voice echoes in the dark. A sugar cube melts in my mouth.

The night flickers with fireflies.

BREAKFAST

Bare children's feet are wet from the dew. They stomp on the embers of last night's bonfire, which retain the power of the fire. We can see the children through the large kitchen window. Grandmother says that ash heals leg and skin ailments and that I should join them so that I don't get scabies. Mother spreads jam on a slice of bread. I can't go out while I'm eating. My brother's already left; the rifle is not in the corner behind the sofa.

Great-Aunt doesn't have a bathroom; like Grandmother, she goes to the privy. It leans against the pigsty next to the garden. I gulp down fresh air in front of the door. I pee as quickly as I can over the black hole. Instead of toilet paper, pieces of old paper bags have been skewered onto a nail. I breathe out the fresh air. I can't hold it any more and breathe in the stench of the black hole. I go out and run through the garden. Bean leaves slash my bare legs, the wet ground sticks to my flip-flops. Dunja's waiting for me on the road. Bekan's coming with us too. Aunt comes out and calls us back into the house. Dunja hasn't eaten anything. She has to eat even though her stomach's been hurting since breakfast and she's feeling nauseous.

※

The house has just been built. The walls are brick, the floors concrete. Rugs and pieces of carpet are spread over the floor. The daughter-in-law's children, who are younger than us, are seated at the table. Dunja and I sit down with them. Aunt leaves the kitchen and disappears behind a curtain, which is actually a piece of fabric threaded onto wire. That's where the pantry is, though it was meant to be a bathroom. She comes back with milk in a large round pan and puts it on the hot stove. It's stifling in the house; there's no fresh air coming in through the open door. She brings out a tall gold tin of luncheon meat and places it on the table. The bread crumbles while she's cutting it. She puts a slice on everyone's plate.

Every month, Aunt moves the button from the waistband of her skirt in by a thumb's width. She cuts the thread with scissors and pulls off the button. Grandmother shakes her head and says that she's as thin as a pin, and if she continues like this she'll wither away altogether. Her eyes are outlined by green crayon. All she has left is a small stub, which she sharpens with a kitchen knife. The stove's fire makes the crayon melt like wax.

The tin has been opened with a knife, so the edges are irregular and sharp. Aunt lifts the lid with her finger. She starts bleeding and a few drops of blood slide down the smooth gold surface. The tin has stood in the pantry for days and the luncheon meat has gone off. There are maggots on the inside surface of the tin. Live grains of rice. She closes the tin without a word and returns it to the pantry so that the daughter-in-law won't think we're ungrateful.

Bits of fatty clotted cream float in the mugs of hot milk. Our stomachs heave at the sight of it. Dunja kicks me under the table. We grab the bread and run outside. We slip on our flip-flops and untie Bekan. We run down the churned-up, dusty road. Aunt yells after us. Her voice fades in our laughter. The bread melts in our mouths.
    We smell of fresh yeast.

SCRAWNY

We're standing on tiptoe on a large rock under our great-aunt's kitchen window. We take turns looking through the hole in the bedsheet, which she covers the window with when she has a bath. She's naked and sitting on a wooden stool, her white fat cascading over the edge. Her legs are spread wide apart, a drooping belly between them. It droops just like her bottom lip does. Her shoulders are narrow, her back hunched, sprinkled with freckles and moles of different shapes and sizes, from an infinite number of warts to large coffee beans. There's a yellow plastic basin of warm water in front of her. She bends over to rinse the rag and her boobs droop all the way to the floor.

Dunja pushes my head away so that she can get a better look. She asks me if we'll look like that one day. She jumps off the rock, hunches her back and stretches the skin on her neck. She pretends she's toothless. She wobbles with pretend fat. We burst out laughing and run towards the riverbank.

Mother washes me in the front yard. She heats water in a laundry pot on the stove, takes it outside and puts it down next to the well, and then mixes hot water with cold water in buckets. I stand on the grass in my swimsuit. It's red, with frills and juicy watermelon slices printed on it. The black pips are the moles on Great-Aunt's back. Boys on bikes are shouting on the road, dry branches and willow switches in their hands. They burst out laughing when they see me. Goran heckles:

'Scrawny!'

A yellow-red chick. That's what I look like. I'm overcome with terrible shame. My mother relentlessly pours water over my head. She doesn't see the tears spilling from my eyes. After the bath, I put on a striped purple outfit. All the girls in the village are wearing the same. We got new ones from Caritas. Made in Germany. Dunja says that prison clothing is also striped; ours is just more cheerful.

Mother has her bath when it gets dark. Grandmother gets angry then. She says that you're not supposed to go outside at dusk without crossing yourself, let alone draw water from a well. Mother throws the bucket into the blackness, and Grandmother murmurs:

> Praise be to Jesus, cold water
> Jesus rule over you forever after

Mother looks completely different then. Like someone else's mother. She wears a very short dress with thin straps. Her breasts and hair are loose. A bucket in one hand, a small pot in the other and a slither of laundry soap. Mother is the only one with long hair; all the other women have short curly hair. There's a hairdresser in the village who has the women come to her house. She puts a stained towel over their shoulders and acid on their hair, and then wraps it around thin curlers. She tightens the curlers with elastic bands. They leave her money and cigarettes. Their hair smells for days after. It dries and becomes hard like old sheep's wool. Aunt cries in front of the mirror; her tears are green.

Mother locks herself in the privy. She takes off her dress in the dark and hangs it from the nail which protrudes from the board. She stands with her legs spread over the black hole. She collects warm water in the little pot and then pours it over her head. The water runs off her hair down her breasts, her legs. It hits the concrete floor and ends up in the black hole. It unsettles the hole, and the stench is unbearable. She can't hear a single blowfly but knows there are whole swarms on the boards above her head.

The riverbank stinks as well. The Bosna is clear, but there is more and more rubbish on the banks. Rusty old stoves, white plastic containers. Dunja hits the water with a stick.

'Have you caught anything?'

I recognise Goran's voice. Pebbles crunch under his wheels.

'Hey! Take it easy!'

He smiles. He takes a soft sweet out of his pocket and lowers it into my hand.
    I break it in half. We smell of melted sugar.

PEACOCKS

The screaming of peacocks can be heard best on a late afternoon when the air in the village settles. The women then sit on old stumps in front of the houses and remain silent. They know that news will arrive soon, and that women's screams will be heard from at least one of the houses. Ilonka and Karlo sit with us every day. He sits on the stump; she squats beside him. We can see up her dress, like when she sits against the wall in front of the school. No matter how hard we try, we can't avert our eyes.

'He's learnt the litany by heart,' Ilonka says.

Karlo starts reciting, gazing into emptiness. We're silent until he finishes, because if we interrupt him he'll have to start from the beginning again.

Lucka, an old maid, bought herself those peacocks. Her house is on a hill, surrounded by a metal fence. She got them when she returned from Germany. She never married.

'She wants to have her own money,' Great-Aunt says. 'She can't eat everything she has, so the food in her house goes off. In the end, it's all thrown to the pigs.'

Dunja and I follow Ilonka and Karlo to Lucka's house. We stand in front of the fence. We've never seen live peacocks, except on the morning television programme, the fairy tale *The Golden Apples and the Nine Peahens*. Dunja says, it's a scam that peahens don't have tails and colours like that. You can read about everything in the encyclopaedia. Neither the apples nor the chickens in Lucka's yard are close to being as beautiful as those on the bedspread in Great-Aunt's room, but the peacocks are much more beautiful in real life. Lucka offers us chocolate and a peacock feather through the fence.

A green eye regards us from above.

CHICKENS

Chop, chop, chop, chop...

Can you hear the blows of the axe on the wooden block? Just wait a minute and you'll smell the scent of hot blood and mud.

Mother is competent. She decapitates the chickens with one stroke. She leaves the heads lying on the wooden block, and the headless feathery bodies end up in a box with a lid. Grandmother holds the lid down until the flapping stops, and then she throws the chickens into boiling water. Great-Aunt submerges them with a stake and then stirs like she's making jam.

When a chicken is left in the rain with its head bent low, we know it's going to die, and then you have to kill them all.

Great-Aunt takes them out of the water with her bare hands, as if the water was cold. She grabs them by the legs and throws them onto the table in front of my mother and brother. Severed veins of different colours stick out of the neck like electric cables. The wet feathers stink worse than the muddy ground under our feet.

Grandmother sticks her knife into a plucked body. She puts the innards into a bowl for soup. She has to cut open the stomachs and wash them. They're yellow and powdery inside.

She throws the intestines into the basin by the table. Sivka and Great-Aunt's cats prowl around it, meowing loudly. Their snouts are red.

Soup is boiling in a pot on the stove. Chicken feet with the claws removed, livers and hearts are cooking in fat. Great-Aunt and Grandmother have packed the meat into buckets with lard and lowered it into the well so that it lasts longer. The white smoke on the walls transforms into black droplets and melts the grime off the walls. Unbearable, stinking heat in the house; outside, red puddles and pieces of chicken innards are covered in blowflies.

Yellow soup in the bowl. Small chicken hearts. Grandmother slurps them off the spoon with the soup; she gobbles them like the gap under the train tracks. She has nothing to chew with; she just swallows and then digests for a long time, like the ground. Grandmother always eats as much as she can.

Otherwise it'll disappear.

Grandmother had a doll as big as Julija. She pressed a button on its back and there was a short, loud cry. It was the only doll in the village that could cry. Next to the doll there was a colourful bag made out of pearls. Grandmother's father bought it for her when she was five years old. Grandmother knows him best from a photo of a man with a moustache and neatly combed hair. He had put on a uniform for it. She was happy he was leaving. He made her play in her room, but she liked to watch the fire burning and her mother making bread on the hearth. A black book with white letters returned instead of her father.

They ate rotting, sprouting potatoes. Grandmother's mother exchanged the doll and bag for flour and sugar, and the children ate well for at least a month. Grandmother eats as much as she can.

'It'll be gone! It'll be gone!'

'I don't have the crying doll or the colourful pearl bag any more.'

The soup goes cold. There's a film of fat as yellow as the wax of a prayer candle on the surface.

LICE

Grandmother stands on the veranda with a pair of big tailor's scissors. She says she has to cut our hair and dust us with pyrethrins like lice-infested chickens. I tie my hair up at the top of my head and run away from Grandmother, even though I know she wouldn't dare and Mother would never let her. I can't resist shouting that she could fall and stab herself with the scissors.

Besides the stench, we also took lice with us from Great-Aunt's house.

The house we have been allocated isn't far from Great-Aunt's, half an hour's walk down the road. Grandmother and Great-Aunt cry while saying their goodbyes. My brother and I are glad we're leaving: we'll have our own rooms. Grandmother uses her headscarf to wipe away her tears. I'm carrying my black suitcase and the hamper with Sivka. She hid behind the sofa, so I had to catch her by the tail. She scratched me and drew blood. Mother goes first, carrying a suitcase and bulging plastic bags. Brother and I follow her, and Grandmother waddles behind us. Great-Aunt stands in the road and watches us until we're out of sight.

The old and never-finished house is in the middle of a wide meadow overrun with weeds and wild flowers. It is the ugliest house in the village. Instead of a proper façade, it has blackened concrete blocks. The gutters are corroded, leaky. Upstairs, instead of windows, it has black holes like gouged-out eyes. The veranda is covered by corrugated blue Salonit tiles. It's hot and dusty underneath. Sawdust spills out of the wooden supports. Grandmother says that you can find worms a finger thick in such timber.

Mother turns the key in the lock and the wooden door scrapes on the concrete. The dark and the damp make her cough. The house squeaks inside. Mice are in the walls, in the furniture, in the holes in the floor. Mother spreads glue over pieces of old plywood and puts bits of rancid bacon on them. The mice stuck to the plywood squeak even louder. Mother throws them onto the rubbish heap behind the house. When she lights it, they stink of fur and meat.

The litter of mice in the cabinet under the sink are eyeless. The red litter are completely transparent. Lift one up to the sun! You can clearly see the intertwining of blue and purple veins and a large, pounding heart. Mother throws them into a bucket, and they fall noiselessly, a small heap of squirming meat. Mother empties the bucket into the canal behind the house. The stagnant water surface is disturbed. The shadows of flaky dandelions fall on it. Soon, the surface is completely still.

We're sitting in the sun. My head is in Mother's lap. She's patiently combing out my hair, lock by lock. Lice and nits pop between her nails.

It's getting dark. Mother and I are tired of the combing. I sit on the veranda and Mother throws a towel over my shoulders.

She dusts my head with pyrethrins. They shouldn't be left on my scalp for long or I'll die. That's how all Grandmother's chickens died once.

Sivka leaves dead mice on the threshold.

THE HOUSE WITH
THE WEEPING WILLOW

Dunja doesn't live near me any more. She's moved to a new house with her mother. A weeping willow grows in front of it. It's as big as the house. Its canopy is our tent. It's always dark beneath it; only during the day does a bit of light penetrate its thick branches. We rarely go into the house, because there are several other families there. It's always crowded in the kitchen. Pots clang, rubber shoes stick to the linoleum. The women are red in the face from the fire in the stove; they open the windows in vain. Particles of flour vibrate in the air and fall on their singed hair and gaunt faces.

The house had been shut up. No one has lived there for a long time. Dunja says that they must be in Germany, because they found newspapers in German in the house, and there is beautiful wallpaper and a thick carpet on the stairs, the likes of which the other houses don't have. The bedrooms are upstairs. One of them is locked. They have been told that they can't go in there. Dunja and I peek through the keyhole. Inside there's black wooden furniture and a crystal chandelier, tablecloths folded on the table, flowered linen and porcelain dishes. Everything of value is locked in the room.

That's why the kitchen contains mismatched plates and bent cutlery.

Dunja's room is in the attic. It's small, just a bed and an old dresser. There's just enough room between them to open the dresser doors. We sit on the floor and look through the crowded shelves. There's so much there: knitting needles, various skeins of wool, plastic dishes, burnt-out light bulbs wrapped in newspaper, tools. Dust sticks to the tips of our fingers. Dunja flicks through a black notebook with cake recipes. The handwriting slants right, the letters small and regular. She reads out loud: Two oranges, sugar, baking powder, vanilla extract, orange liqueur, whipped cream, a fruit of your choice...

Our stomachs rumble, our mouths water. I take a half-empty bag of coconut flour from the dresser, its scent faded a long time ago. We lick our dusty fingers and push them into the coconut flour bag. We swallow thick saliva dusted with flavourless flakes.

PRISONERS

We're sitting under the weeping willow, our backs against the trunk. Bekan is lying on the grass at our feet and napping. For days now, Dunja has been carrying around a yellow book with a singed cover. Uncle brought it from somebody's home library. It's the love story of Peter and Miet. She reads it out loud:

Miet raised her hand, responding with weak movements. Then, realising that the train was still moving slowly and that she would be able to keep up with it, she hurried after the carriage and extended her hand to Peter.
Peter leant out from the steps.
'Be careful that you don't trip...'
He gently caught the hand she extended to him, and Miet took several steps alongside the train. But she had to quicken her pace more and more, and finally their hands parted.

Dunja says that we're going to say goodbye to our lovers like this one day. We'll wear black coats to look like widows and wipe our tears carefully with ironed handkerchiefs.

PHANTASMA

Sit with me on the roof of the red Lada! Be careful! It's as hot as the train tracks.

On my head, I've got my father's cap, which is wet around the rim from sweat. It's too big, and I hold it with my hand so that it doesn't fall over my eyes. The Lada is parked in the middle of the road. My father is standing in front of me, his head bare. The sun is merciless; it fries his bald head, droplets of sweat glistening. His face is hidden by a large camera. A Polaroid. Father has Grandmother's features: tiny black eyes, colourless eyebrows and a pear-shaped nose. They even have the same wart on the inner corner of the left eye, thin lips and a round head. The only difference is that Father, like Grandfather, has good teeth. My brother and I love Father's camera because the photos come out of it the moment you click. First, they're completely green, like the screen of a turned-off television, and then, slowly, blurry contours and human silhouettes emerge. Only then do the colours and tiny details appear. Our display cabinet is full of photos. Thick albums and shoeboxes crammed with photos are in the drawers. The ones Mother likes best are arranged on the glass panes of the display cabinet and propped up against the ornate glasses, which are only used if we have guests from far away. We usually take photos on Sundays. Mother dresses us in fine clothes and positions us among the roses.

Through the lens, Father sees me resting on my arms on the hot roof, the cap slipping over my eyes, and Sivka, who jumped up after me, with her tail raised high. The veranda can be seen in the background. Grandmother is sitting on her stool looking at the knitting in her hands. Mother is looking at us, smiling and wiping her hands on her apron.

The photo comes out of the camera. Father waves it around as if he's drying it. Sivka and I jump off the roof. She disappears into the grass, and I take the photo from my father's hands. On the green surface, blurry contours and yellow stains emerge. The red colour of the car and my white hair, which falls over my shoulders, all the way down to the roof. The colours mix. Sivka and I are twinned transparent contours. A black hole instead of my smile. My eyes are not visible under the cap. Behind us nothing is discernible, neither the veranda nor Mother.

The photograph is blurry. A quivering phantasm.

Mother is disappointed. She turns the photo in her hands as if expecting to find a fault she can fix. Father says the film is old and that he can't get a new roll now.

Mother sticks the photograph to the glass pane in the display cabinet in the hall.

BLOWFLY

Mother has already got up. The impression of her body is still in the bed beside me; it doesn't smell of roses and sugared boiled milk any more. Great-Aunt's house has infused us with the smell of soot, rancid oil and damp. There are long black hairs on the pillow.

The morning is completely quiet. I can't hear the clanging of pots or the rustling of bags in the hall, even though I know that Mother and Grandmother are getting ready to go home. We're staying one more day. The summer has come to an end, and now the gardens and orchards are overripe. If it rains, everything will rot. We don't have any winter stores anyway. We're going to make tomato sauce. They told us it was peaceful and safe in our village, but we have to get home before dark.

I can see from my bed that the window is open, although the curtains are drawn. They're full of birds with sharp beaks flying towards the ground and flowers blossoming upside down. Someone has sewed them badly. A blowfly alights on the pillow between Mother's hairs. The hairs are the blowfly's long legs and they've taken up the whole pillow.

Can you see its red eyes getting larger?

I bring my hand down on the pillow. The blowfly briefly buzzes by my ear and disappears.

I get up and open the curtains. The hooks scrape along the rusty rail, like eyelashes on a pillowcase. The birds and flowers disappear. The clouds are pink, airy cotton candy, and above them a tranquil red sky. Grandmother says that a red sky in the morning forecasts bad weather, but it's calm. Crows are flying over the fields in large flocks, and our forest is distant and dark.

My dress is draped over the chair. The white, worn-out cotton is like the gauze through which Mother strains soup. I can see myself from head to foot in the mirror next to the wardrobe. I'm nearly as tall as Mother. I'm already taller than Grandmother. My hair and skin are as white as the feathers in Mother's pillow. Field fenugreeks on my chest. I tie the dress with knots at the shoulders.

The front door is open. Mother has put all the suitcases and hampers on the floor in the hall. We're ready to leave. We don't take anything but the pots and jars. I'll take Sivka too, because I'm afraid that she may think we've abandoned her and that she'll get lost if she tries to find us. Grandmother is sitting on the veranda in a flower-print dress and the black sandals she wears to church. Sivka jumps into the hamper.

My brother loads the suitcases and hampers into the trunk. He's still walking around naked to the waist. Mother gives him his T-shirt; he just crumples it and throws it into the car.

Mother and I sit in the back. Sivka is between us. Grandmother gets in and the red Lada rocks.

My brother turns the key and the engine springs to life. Grandmother crosses herself.

III

UNWASHED QUINCES

There's no room for you in the old Lada. Peek through the window! Grandmother is taking up all the space and breathing up all the air. She wipes sweat off her face and bald head with her headscarf. Dust and bits of yellow foam spill from the torn seats and stick to our damp skin. Our hands are freshly picked hairy quinces.

We don't open the windows because clouds of soft golden dust rise from the country road. Grandmother pants louder than she did when she was leading me by the hand over the railway bridge. She grips the handle above the window. Her fingers are as white as my brother's on the steering wheel. He's only sixteen and hasn't passed his driving test yet, but Father lets him drive in the village. We all get out of his way, and he only got stuck in the garden once, in Grandmother's potato patch.

Mother is quiet, her gaze occupied by the withered cornfields and sunflowers. The yellow turns into orange in the late afternoon. A murder of crows take off from the riverbank and land on the stalks, their claws gripping the dry corn. You can hear them scratching the rough leaves with their claws like spruce needles, pecking the half-dry, sun-scorched yellow grains. Mother can't see what's disturbed the birds; they caw loudly, rise into the air and line up on the cables above the train track. Her fingers squeeze the flower petals on the hem of her dress. A blowfly buzzes near my ear. I wave my hand, and it disappears in Mother's hair. It shimmers neon green and blue. A drop of sweat on my hairline is cold well water.

The country road follows the snaking train tracks overgrown with wild angelica, dark berries and danewort. The village is visible from the railway crossing. The trees seem to have doubled, the forest to have descended to the road. I would be able to touch it if I opened the window and extended my arms. We go over the crossing and I open the window. It's still dusty. Mother grabs me by the hand. I can feel the heat pulsing under her skin. Grandmother yells at me not to stick my head through the window – I'd fall out and be dead on the spot.

The Lada races along the road for a short distance and then turns between the two tall pine trees onto our dirt track and stops between our house and Grandmother's. I can see Aunt standing on a chair, washing the windows. Grandmother wipes her head one more time and exhales. We're going to suffocate if we don't open a window soon. I hurry to get out because I'm scared that even Sivka can't breathe. Aunt sees us and waves. Across the road, Ilonka and Karlo are stacking logs to saw. They shout when they speak.

Grandfather comes out of the cellar. He's as unkempt as the hedge and the forest. I can't make out his face among his hair, eyebrows and beard. He is as dark and cold as the cellar.

Grandmother thinks he's the same as he was that day in the photo studio: straight back, broad shoulders, a canopy on his head, sharp blades of grass breaking through his shirt.

Grandmother folds her headscarf into a triangle and puts it on her head. She has never pulled the knot tighter.

CAMOMILE FLOWERS

Mother takes the curtains off the windows in the kitchen and living room. As we're home, she'll freshen up the house. The once white lace is black from time and the smoke of the oil lamp. The bathtub is full of warm water, which Mother has brought in pots from the summer kitchen. We soak the curtains, and the water turns dark instantaneously. We rub them with pieces of laundry soap, black water running down our hands, stinking of smoke and dust. The lace is becoming lighter and softer, as thin as Grandmother's veil in the wedding portrait. We rinse them in cold well water. My skin goes red; the chill seeps down to the bone. Mother hangs them out on the line in the meadow above the house. It's supported in the middle by a long forked pole. Sunlight and the scent of soap mingle.

Julija and I are lying on the extended sofa. My throat still hurts from Father's fingers. Mother and I have stopped crying. She's hidden all the hard-boiled sweets. She won't give any to me or my brother, even though he swears he'll eat sitting up. We sleep in; the sun rose a long time ago. There are no curtains in the living room window, only the forest and white lace on the washing line in the shiny pane. I get up and go barefoot into the yard, Julija under my arm. We charge into the lace and the white sheets fluttering in the air. They smell different to clothing that's been washed with laundry soap, of white washing powder and the wild flowers from the pink bottle of fabric softener. My wedding veil is going to smell the same. The veil will flutter in my wedding picture, as thin as breath. We lie down on the grass. Up there, high in the sky, a white line forms. Julija and I shout:

> Plane, plane, up so high,
> drop us sweets from the sky.

The bathroom is warm from the steam and Mother's sweat. There's some water left, and Mother brings a small saucepan from the kitchen. I untie my hair and lean over the bathtub. Mother pours water over me, scrubs me with laundry soap as if I were the curtains, until I squeak under her fingers. She brings a jar with dry camomile flowers from the pantry. She shakes them into a basin and pours boiling water over them. She cools the infusion and washes my hair with it. It's going to make my hair as white as bone. I wrap my head in a towel. I close the jar and return it to the pantry shelf. It's always dark in there because it's under the stairs and has no window, and the light bulb next to the front door is useless now. The pantry smells like it did before, of caramel, lemon rind and vanilla sugar. Like the period leading up to Christmas.

I stand on tiptoe and switch the light on in the pantry. I leave Julija on the stairs. Pieces of sugared quinces and black cherries float in jars on the highest shelf, which Mother serves in small crystal bowls, with coffee. Pickled peppers and grated cabbage are on the shelves below. There are also tiny green tomatoes and big cucumbers. There are Christmas biscuits under a dishcloth on the table, which smell of lard and sugar. The fritters leave traces of icing sugar on my fingertips. Lemon squares and chocolate cake under a plastic lid. My stomach is full. I wipe my mouth and fingers on my dress. Julija looks at me from the doorway, but she won't betray me.

I unfold a chair above the house, next to the washing line with the curtains. I take off the wet towel and comb my hair, which smells of camomile. My hair dries quickly in the sun. It rustles like the lace, dry snow from the fields.

APPLES

The bear's paw scrapes over Grandfather's beard, sandpaper on old wood.

'Come here!'

The cellar door is wide open. The stench of rakija, damp and dust radiates from inside. A heap of dirty dishes is on the table along the wall, dried-up leftovers on plates, greasy forks and knives, breadcrumbs all over the place. Grandfather's dirty clothes are on Grandmother's sofa, and crumpled linen on the other one. When he doesn't have to be on guard duty, Grandfather sleeps in the cellar. During the day, he supervises the digging of trenches.

Beside the display cabinet, the smell of rakija is stronger. The bottles lined up against it are empty, their tops scattered over the floor. Grandfather knocks them over with his foot and swears. He opens the glass door on the cabinet and takes out two apples, the first to have fallen from the branches this year.

'Take them. Give one to Dunja.'

Dunja, Julija and I sit beneath the apple tree. The bench is our bus. Dunja drives us from one city to another, Zagreb, Ljubljana, Belgrade. When we move out, we'll go there together. We'll sit on hotel terraces in city centres in beautiful dresses and shoes with bows, eat cakes and listen to music. Big city streets are spacious, with fountains and avenues. We can forget about muddy, churned-up roads.

In the dark of the cellar, Grandfather's teeth flash, his green eyes flash. Grandfather gets taller, he's broken through the ceiling, filled out the whole cellar. The whole roof will crash down on us. I grab the apples and run out of the cellar.

The sun takes the cold and dark from me. I run down the road to Dunja.

The thick, warm juice explodes in our mouths.

BLACKBERRIES

There's splashing behind us in the swamp, spattering our bare skin. Dunja taps on the bottom of the plastic basin like a drum. Her hands are thin, like the white lines on the blue vest. She takes a turtle out of the bushes near the tracks. It pulls its head into its shell on her palm. The turtles in the basin are like black rocks. We leave them near the train tracks. They push their heads out and try to climb the plastic walls, unsuccessfully. The tracks are infinitely long. We take off our flip-flops and walk along the track like on a beam. The hot iron scorches us; we have to be quicker. I don't last long; I put my flip-flops back on. The rubber sole is soothing on the skin. Dunja speeds along; I can't keep up.

Purple irises and wild gladioli blossom along the tracks in early spring. They remind me of bouquets of large butterflies. We don't have a car at the moment, so we walk to the neighbouring village along the tracks: it's much closer than by road. Mother and I walk in front of Father and my brother. She holds my hand and lifts it as I jump from sleeper to sleeper. There's a train behind us; it's still far away, but we can feel the ballast tremble. We get off the track and stand by the hedge. The rumble is ever stronger. The engine whistles. Mother and Father open their coats. My brother and I hide in the warm darkness, in silence. The world outside the coat roars.

Blackberries drop onto the palms of our hands at a touch. We only pick those exposed to the sun. The hedge is cold inside and hisses. Our hands are blue and sticky. Tart and sweet juice glides down our throats. Fingerprints on white cotton, which won't come off in the wash.

Dunja is a newborn mouse in the sun. I can see every one of her veins underneath her thin skin. If I could lift her up towards the sun, I'm sure I'd be able to see her heart beating. She's laughing. Her teeth are red from the berries, like Sivka's when she leaves a dead mouse in front of the door.

Trains haven't passed this way for a long time. I have to close my eyes to feel the rumble.

At school, we read a story about a blind boy whose house is by the tracks, and he's used to the rumble of trains. He stands in front of his house and waves to the passengers. He doesn't know that they wave back. I wonder what the world would be like in the dark. For the blind boy, it might always be as it was for me in Mother's coat. I stand in the swamp and wait for the next train. I close my eyes and wave. I'm curious, so I peek through my eyelashes. No one waves back from the windows.

We sit on the ballast in front of old Feriz's house. Two grey cats are resting there. Their bodies are thin, their breathing slow. The windows on the house are covered with white sheets. The door's closed. The glass pane on the door has cracked diagonally and is held together by brown Sellotape. Yellow dandelions stick out of concrete which has been cracked by rain. The dry cornfield behind the house doesn't rustle. It's motionless and mute, soldiers standing to attention. Sleek crows are lined up on the black electricity cable behind the haystack.

CHICKS

The box in Grandmother's hands chirps. Sharp three-toed claws scratch at old newspapers. Rusty sardine tins are full of water and cornflour. Grandmother takes a chick and puts it on the palm of my hand. A bulrush flake. The fragile feet are cold and sharp. Grandmother hides the chicks from rats, which can eat a small chicken. We're all afraid of rats. Even Grandfather.

Instead of mice, a rat wriggles out from under the rotten floorboards in the bedroom. It's as big as a rabbit. Grandmother's on the bed, motionless. Grandfather's growling. The rat is cornered and spitting. It has nowhere to go. Grandfather feels a weight on his trouser legs. He stamps his feet on the floor. It's already on his shoulder, on his neck. It bites him with its long, sharp teeth. Grandfather screeches. The bear's paw beats the air.

Grandmother shakes with laughter on the bed, her two gold teeth shining.

Grandmother wipes away her tears.

'Make sure Sivka doesn't kill them.'

IN THE BOILING CAULDRON

Mother is picking tomatoes in the garden. Her legs are dusty to the knees, to the hem of her dress. The stems and leaves of the tomato plants are yellow and wilted; you can barely detect the strong smell that emanates from them when they're fresh, but they're still prickly. The tomatoes are of different sizes, colours and shapes, from light green to yellow to dark red. Bucketfuls of them. Mother throws the large rotting heads onto a heap at the edge of the garden. They burst and spill. Ah, here come the blowflies! Can you hear the buzzing? They land on the spilt heap. It's already as black as a mound of earth.

My brother has lit a fire under the cauldron in front of the house. Catching, it crackles and licks the sides of the cauldron. Even though he has spent the whole summer going around without a shirt on, he is as white as a lily petal. I've washed the old jam jars and turned them upside down to dry on the old tablecloth. When they're completely dry, I line them up in rows on a tray and put them in the hot oven to heat up.

Mother sits by the house with her dress hitched up, a bucket filled with red juice between her spread legs. Seeds and bits of tomato skin float on the surface. There are tomatoes in a black bowl of water; the knife in Mother's hand cuts through the overripe, bruised flesh. It gets under her fingernails, red droplets trickle down to her elbows. Her hair shimmers. The buzzing is ever louder. My brother empties a full bucket of diced tomatoes into the cauldron and stirs it with a piece of wood. The juice quickly comes to the boil and thickens. Air struggles to break through to the surface. Hot droplets of sauce spit from the cauldron like from a volcano and fall on the dry, thinned grass. Insects and ants flee as if from a fire.

Mother fills the jars that have just been taken out of the oven; the clean glass shines in the sun. She covers the mouths of the jars with cellophane and then screws the lids on tightly. I put them away in the pantry.

Grandmother brings a tray of coffee cups out to the table under the apple tree.

THE ROAR

Get ready! We're running out of time. The silence and summer lethargy will not last long.

Deep in the forest, it's dark and cold even in the summer. The ground is black and damp, the moss a green carpet. Footsteps are inaudible there. The soft flight of the night owl. Its strong strokes swirl the air into a whirlwind. Birds, foxes and rabbits flee from it. The flesh of poisonous mushrooms squelches under the ribbed sole of tightly laced boots. Pine trees emit seductive sweet scents, their sap is as warm and sticky as the hot drops of a prayer candle. In the darkness of the forest, eyes are mute. Open wide.

Their footsteps rustle at the edge of the forest, in the dense undergrowth chilled by hemlock. Among the chestnuts and oaks, the air is lighter, airy and shimmering. It's cut by a hellish roar which is reminiscent of the roar of the Bosna between the train tracks, of the roar of the monsters in Ilonka's stories.

The sky parts with the first sparks and smell of gunpowder. Bird wings vanish in the smoke, like in the thick mist of early morning. Grandfather's bear's paw grabs Grandmother's elbow. Grandmother is heavy and clumsy, stumbling in front of the cellar. Her flip-flops slip off. Grandfather locks the door. Cups of undrunk coffee remain under the apple tree.

There's a half-sawn log in front of Ilonka's house, the metal saw still stuck in the log. Karlo's milk mug is on the concrete in front of the door. Ilonka and Karlo have locked themselves in the house, in the wardrobe. It's too tight for both of them. The black baize of old coats drops over their heads. Their breath mingles. Ilonka grips Karlo; she can't calm his quivering body. Boys are thin branches, afraid of storms. They can't do anything about them. Litanies flow from Karlo's mouth.

Mother grips the hem of her dress. She knows it's already too late. She doesn't recognise the voices coming from the street. She turns round in the yard, but she can't see me or my brother. She runs into the house.

I was four, my brother was six. We were sitting in the dark, in the woodshed. We had broken a bottle of strawberry syrup in the kitchen. The thick syrup had spread over the tiles and the rug. We had stepped into it barefoot, and left footprints all over the house. Mother would yell at us. We could hear her calling. We remained sitting in the dark because if we had come out then, she would have fetched a willow switch. Grandmother was calling too. Mother's voice was trembling. She started crying. We were crying too.

They've already spread out over the village. The women in the yards of the houses by the forest haven't got away. They're forcing them to walk ahead of them. The women hold their children's hands tightly.

They've descended all the way to the tracks. The birds on the black cable above Feriz's house spread their wings and disappear into their nests under the roofs. The cats dart up the tall walnut tree. The cornfield behind the house starts rustling and the stalks come crashing down one by one.

They're as quick as the maggots in the luncheon-meat tin. The interiors of the houses tremble with echoes and curses. They bang on walls. Bodies squeeze in under beds, behind doors, in wardrobes and pantries. All in vain. They pull them out like rabbits out of a bush.

Male bodies are powerful, they don't hesitate. The charge is fervent and loud. It parches the throat. There's no water in the houses. Bowls full of tomatoes are on the tables in the kitchens. They bite into them, the membranes burst. Red juice sprinkled with seeds spurts. They throw the half-eaten tomatoes onto the floor, the hearts trampled.

CONCRETE DUST

Fear is cold on the outside even though its innards are boiling hot. Its lips pale and dry. Its forehead cooled by dew. Eyes open wide from the swearing and saliva that spread over the face of fear. Its hearing is sharper. The ear shatters from unknown sounds. It's clear that the creak on the stairs and the clang of metal are announcing death.

But the song is so soft. Cat's paws on carpet.

> Get up, darling, my beauty, come
> The rain has stopped, winter is gone.

'Don't let anyone hear you,' Mother says.

The women in the village wear black. They drink calamint tea in the mornings. Dunja says we're lucky because we have calamint in abundance. It grows like weeds near the swamp. Women pick it on sunny days when it has dried because damp flowers decay quickly. They spread them out on clean sheets. Grandmother says that it cures sorrow. You just have to drink it regularly.

The kitchen is full of sun. The windows are still curtainless. The curtains are still hanging on the clothesline above the house. I take the broom from behind the door and raise a thick, trembling cloud.

If the clock worked, it would show five o'clock.

Mother's hand is rough. She's gripping me by the wrist and dragging me through the dark hallway and then up the stairs to the first floor. The emptiness echoes. We don't say a thing. We lie on the floor against the wall. Our cheeks on the bumpy concrete. Fine concrete dust scrapes our nostrils. My brother's not here. He's still downstairs. Can't he hear that the sky has crashed down on us? Mother puts her arm across my back. But you can't save your child with an embrace. She's not crying, but her eyes are glistening with bubbles. My eyes are spilling tears. The puddle is tiny. It remains on the surface. The dust won't let it be soaked up by the cold concrete. A downpour on the tin roof. Hail. We can't hear the doves cooing.

My brother and a soldier with a black sash around his head look at each other through the large window in the kitchen. For a fraction of a second. His face is etched in my brother's brain. He's young. Eyes of coal, a patchy beard. His long, wet hair flutters with the black sash. The bullet misses my brother. It breaks the glass and lodges itself in the back of the green armchair. My brother flees through the dark hallway. The soldier with the black sash is waiting for him at the open front door.

'Hands behind your head!'

My brother is standing on the threshold. He's naked to the waist. Breathing hard and pale. His chest heaving. The light hairs under his armpits are wet, rivers of sweat run from them. My brother sees Grandfather behind the soldier with the black sash. The green eye aims. Grandfather's bear's paw never wavers. The coal eyes of the soldier widen for a split second, his mouth opens, his rifle falls to the concrete. He staggers and crumples into a heap. Grandfather disappears into the cellar. A fraction of a second. My brother's not even sure he ever stood in front of the cellar. The soldier falls face down on the ground. There is a large hole in his back, his shirt is singed. His blood is thick and black, and it spills over the concrete. The door is still open. Mother and I can hear my brother climbing the stairs. He skips several steps. Our hearts pound against the concrete. We breathe rapidly. My brother lies down on the floor. Our insides are full of dust and fear.

A woman's voice calls Mother. Ever louder:

'Come out! They won't hurt you!'

Mother recognises the voice of the woman from the village. My brother says not to go down. Mother's hair shimmers more and more; it buzzes more loudly. Her face becomes darker. Patches erupt on her skin, like on rainy days.

Silence prevails and the glass panes quieten down too.

We can hear them clearly. Heavy footsteps on the wooden stairs. The wood never creaks like that. Metal clangs. My mother and brother get up. I can see Mother's bare feet and my brother's trainers.

And black boots tied very tightly.

This can only be Death.

'Get up!!!'

The sound is painful. You can't pull it out of your ear. It's more painful than a blade in the flesh.

But the song is so soft. Cat's paws on carpet.

> Flowers are blooming, doves are cooing
> The time has come to sing.

STAR-SHAPED FLOWERS

Death is standing behind me. Mother squeezes my hand. She's going to break every bone. We're barefoot, our shoes left lying on the concrete beneath the window, where the scents of concrete dust and camomile flowers mingle. There's dark blood on the threshold. Someone has taken the soldier away, his black sash is still beside the puddle. We step into the puddle in our bare feet like we did into the thick, sticky strawberry syrup. We leave tracks behind us. The smells here are very different. I can't smell concrete or dust, just iron, sweat and smoke.

Can you feel cold fear on your forehead?

Old, hanging faces are already lined up on the road, their hands behind their heads.

And summer... is still calm and quivering. Would the earth quaking and opening up save us? What if lightning were to ignite the dry grass, hedges and trees in the fields? If stormy winds were to rise and throw dust in our eyes? We would be equally small then. Death and I.

Drool spills from their mouths like chained-up wild dogs. Their voices flay our bodies. Their breath is as deep and cold as the cellar. Their insides are as rotten as old potatoes.

My brother's voice is that of a child. The knife glints at his throat. Spit and curses spray his face. His eyes are open wide and mute. He doesn't think he can feel anything, just the touch of metal on his skin. A boy with a knife at his throat is a thin branch in a gale-force wind.

The black boot sends the box with the chicks flying into the air, high up, all the way to the roof. Like Dunja and I leaping over the bonfires. Yellow flakes in the air. He stomps on them, one by one. He transforms them into yellow-red star-shaped flowers.

There is less and less air. Our breaths are wheezes. Short and dry. Bird claws, sharp, hungry beaks grip our backs. Fire strikes the backs of our heads.

Silence in the blink of an eye.

Death emerges from under Grandmother's apple tree, hissing, his foot leaning against the wooden bench. The rose petals along the barbed-wire fence open completely. An army of ants descends on the sugar cubes.

TELL SUMMER THAT I DIED

> When gladness sweeps the land,
> And to the white sky
> Cool butterflies go by,
> And sheep in shadow stand;
> When Love, the old command,
> Turns every hate aside,
> In the unstinted days
> Tell Summer that I died.
>
> JOHN SHAW NEILSON,
> 'Tell Summer that I Died'

Stop for a second! One more second!

Look at his face. This can't be the face of Death. It's pale and tender, a scar above his lip. Death is a boy. His mother is calling him, and he is extending his arms to her.

He's running.

His feet stumble over the rocks in the yard. He's still far away, his mother can't catch him.

Mummy! Mummy!

Round fruit flush above his head, as golden as the fruit on the bedspread on the wall of Great-Aunt's bedroom. His eyes are shadowed. Will his cap fall off and reveal his eyes? Can he see us clearly in the hot, muggy air? Are we just blurry spots to him? A failed photo from my father's Polaroid?

I'm the shortest in the row. All heads turn towards me, like flowers towards the sun. I'm standing between my mother and brother. I'm touching them with my elbows. My brother's hot, naked skin and Mother's flower-print dress. We're trapped. There's nowhere to run. Merciless spruce branches at our backs. They have no canopy to hide in. They're pressing into our backs and our bare arms raised behind our heads. Blossoming barbed wire in front. And a red-hot metal barrel.

Death bends his back a little, closes his eyes and cold teeth.

Mummy! Mummy!

I run into her open coat. Into the scent of dry flowers. Into the warm silence.

At dawn, when it's chilly, Mother squeezes my hand in her pocket.

Crisp biscuits melt in my mouth, with warm milk. Fingers smell of coconut flour.

I must hide!

Under the table! Under the bed! In the pantry! In the dark! Roll into a ball and close my eyes.

No one will be able to find me.

In the coat! In the warm silence!

Death's lips are pale. His index finger is used to the touch of metal. He doesn't waver.

The petals of Grandmother's overblown roses fall onto the grass from the screaming and rain of fire. They rot there in a second. Can you hear the bodies falling with a thud onto the dusty road? Their poses are unimaginable. The dead don't close their eyes. They get stuck like Julija's.

I was hit by one spark. Directly in the heart. Mother hears me calling her.

Mummy! Mummy!

Softly, like the tenderest of songs. She doesn't know that I'm shouting.

You'll go deaf from my screams!

They flood the forest and the fields.

Can you hear them?

They're in the flapping of bird wings, in the wind howling through open windows, in the creaking of wood underfoot, in the clanging of metal.

My camomile hair spread on the road, its light extinguished. My eyes are two dark-blue marbles. The sky is the last thing I see, poisoned by smoke and unknown voices.

Grandmother's mourning headscarf is placed on me.

Mother's hair has fanned out in thick swarms of large blowflies.

They feast on our open wounds.

Does Summer know?

Will it send at least one butterfly, instead of them?

Has anyone told Summer that I died?

ANGEL

You need a break. I know.

Your throat is contracting, yearning for fresh air. Open the windows or stretch out in the shade under a thick treetop in your front garden. Take off your clothes and jump into the lake or river. Transform into a fish and disappear under the surface.

Forget for a moment, but just for a moment. Nothing is over yet. Move back, so you can see better. Look, even the smoke has dispersed.

Our road looks like a field after a storm. Hundreds of flashes of lightning have struck it. Rain and hail have flattened all the plant stems. Broken, burnt, crumpled, torn. All the juice has dripped out of them. Here is a chance for you to see what hides within.

We're strewn about in a disorderly fashion, like when you throw a fistful of corn to the chickens. You'll notice me straight away. White hair. White skin. White dress. Mother will claim later that the stain on my chest looked like a flower. A big red flower.

A white angel with a flower on her chest.

Does the red stain on my chest look like a flower to you?!

Nor to me. It's scorched skin. Blood which has turned black on cotton as thin as gauze. Broken bone and torn lungs. A burst heart.

Have a look! Everything has been knocked over and is motionless; only Death stands tall under Grandmother's apple tree. We still can't see his eyes under his tilted cap.

THE GREEN EYE

In the dark, Grandmother has become a ball of black yarn thrown between the sofa and the wooden display cabinet. She is lamenting helplessly. Fear shrinks her body. People don't have shells like turtles to hide their heads in. All they can do is just tuck their necks in a little, bow their heads and cover their ears with their hands. The cellar walls strain under the weight of the screams and swearing that penetrate through the open window. The wooden display cabinet trembles, the glasses clink.

Grandfather is at one window and then at the other. He says nothing. All flashes of lightning and curses spark in his eye. Grandmother hears them even when they're silent. Only the lightning that strikes the fields is louder and more determined. The louder the thunder, the quieter and quicker Grandmother prays. Words must be quick; they can't be left hovering in the air, lest they crumble like dust.

Grandfather's bear's paw simultaneously pulls both triggers. He fires two lead slugs through the hole between the sandbags. They're faster than Grandmother's prayers. They lodge themselves in Death's tender face. He collapses onto the grass next to the wooden bench. The cap falls off his head.

Death also has dark-blue eyes. Look! The golden fruit of Grandmother's apple tree quiver in his irises, the rustling leaves tremble. Fresh wounds are hot. Cooled black coffee trickles off the plastic tablecloth and into them.

Death is a boy again.

Mummy! Mummy!

KALEIDOSCOPE

Close your eyes, the living among the dead!
Inhale deeply and control your limbs. The break is only momentary.

Black Queen, one, two, three...!

My brother sees a scratched black boot through his eyelashes. It steps into my blood. My hair. He feels someone's breath on his neck, bent in so close.

'They're all finished here!'

That's what he said. My brother knows this well. The words boom in his head. Creaking! Clanging! They're an unswallowed bite, a hard-boiled sweet lodged in the throat.

A few pebbles fly out from under the boot and hit him in the face. He opens his eyes. The voices become more distant. They're already near the forest. They march the other side's living away before them. They carry their dead on their backs.

My brother first sees a long, dirtied lock of my hair and then my unmoving face. He squeezes his eyes shut and then opens them as if everything will disappear with the next blink. He gets up on his knees.

It was summer. My brother was ten. Poles had arrived in the village like they did every year and parked on our playground. They opened the trunks of their cars and set up small tents. They sold everything like at a fair. Clothes, toys, baubles. Mother bought me pink trousers and a small plastic kaleidoscope. I carried it around my neck. I would lie down on the grass in the garden and turn it towards the sun. The colours would change: yellow and red, blue and green, purple. The most beautiful tapestry I had ever seen. My brother pulled it off my neck and ran away. I cried till nightfall.

The images swirl before my brother's eyes at an inconceivable speed. Whose cruel hand is this?

Stuck dark-blue eyes.

Fanned-out hair.

White cotton soaked in blood.

Blown-out lungs.

Bits of brain in hot puddles.

Holes in breasts.

Broken bones.

His eyes mist over. Everything has turned into a bloody watercolour!

His pain tears at his hair. His scream is as loud as the roar of the train. Mother opens her eyes and grabs him by the arm.

'Lie down! They'll kill you too!'

My brother looks at his arms, spread wide. They're covered in blond hairs.

He touches his chest. All the blood on it is someone else's. He is unharmed.

Mother's right leg is riddled with bullet holes.

The air starts exploding again. He lies down and covers his head with his arms. He crawls. There's yellow dirt under his fingernails. He is bruised and scratched all over. My brother's hands leave red prints on the walls of our house. He stumbles and overturns things. A box falls out of the wardrobe. Rolls of white cotton. Cold scissors. He goes back to Mother and bandages her leg.

Mother can't feel her legs or body. She can't move. She extends her arms towards me but can't reach me.

For a moment she closes her eyes and rocks me in her arms.

Mother smells of roses and sweetened boiled milk again.

RED ROSES

Grandfather comes out of the cellar, while Grandmother is still rolled up in a ball between the display cabinet and sofa. My grandfather and brother load Mother onto a wheelbarrow. My brother pushes her down the road to Dunja's house. Help has already arrived there. One moment, Mother sees a bit of sky, my brother's sweaty face and closed eyes, and the next everything goes black before her eyes and her body completely gives way.

They load the wounded onto doors, which have been taken off their hinges, and horizontal ladders instead of stretchers. The holes in the bodies are closed with crumpled T-shirts and shirts, wounds bandaged with torn cotton. The medical field station is down there, below the train tracks.

Grandmother gets up and peers out of the window that looks onto our road.

Spilt blood never cools. My brother was kneeling in a puddle of blood next to me, but not touching me. His hands are shaking as if they've just been lashed by a switch. He tries to lower them to my face. Can stuck eyes be closed? They still shine like marbles turned towards the sun.

I can't hear anything except my brother.

He lets out a scream like Grandfather, deep and dark. Tears run down his face, and drip from his chin to his chest, leaving wet white tracks, snaking like a worm. His hands cover my face. His skin is as if scorched and he cannot feel the touch of my skin. He manages to close my eyes only halfway. They're left half-open, like dark-blue lips.

He picks me up in his arms, like when I grazed my knee on the tip of the green rock. My hair hangs down over his arms. My brother's temple is pulsing, his eyes blossoming with burst capillaries, like when you touch the thin ice on puddles with your boot.

Grandmother has come out of the cellar and is sitting on the well. She's grieving quietly. Nothing's left of her prayers. Grandfather's bear's paw rests on her shoulder.

The withered sunflowers look on as we pass. The burnt-out suns of a late summer. My brother's legs don't give way at all. He lowers me onto the grass, where I used to sunbake with Dunja on large beach towels and where we would listen to the sounds made by the large shells from the display cabinet with the crystal.

The door to the house is open. My brother takes the curtain down from the kitchen window. In it, our forest is on fire. Colours melt on his face. It glistens as if he were getting ready to leap over the burning bonfire. The curtain smells of soap and fresh air. He takes it outside into the yard and wraps me in lace roses.

They bloom red in no time.

BIRDS

A rain of burning suns has descended on our forest, on the fragrant black pine trees. Fire is a gentle lover. It hisses and slithers along the spines of tall pines. It swallows birds' nests in one bite. It transforms newly hatched birds into ash. Black cotton. The night wind disperses it over the village, over thick bloody puddles and silenced roofs.

Instead of flowers.

OVER THE BOSNA

'The army's coming!'

That's all that Dunja hears. She sees her mother peeking from behind the curtain drawn across the kitchen window, which looks out onto the road, onto our house and Grandmother's house. She can see them descending from the upper side of the village, onto the road and our dirt track. She can't make out the words, the echo of unfamiliar voices in her ears. They ring in her head, shake the glass in the windows. They lock the door and hide under the staircase in the hall. Dunja doesn't cry, but her face changes colour. Red turns to purple, purple turns to green. It remains the light green of unripe tomatoes.

Fear trembles in Aunt's voice.

'Everything's going to be OK. If they come, you just be quiet.'

Dunja's hands shake, like when you fall onto icy concrete. Her teeth chatter.

The front door is metal, with small glass panes. The pounding of fists.

'Open up! Open up!'

Aunt gets up and peeks out. She knows every soldier. They're not in uniform, but they have rifles. The military base is in an abandoned house in the village. One of them is lying in front of the door. He's been wounded in the leg and is bleeding on the concrete. Dunja can't take her eyes off the wound. Aunt squeezes her hand. They press up against the wall of the house. One of the soldiers shoots towards the road, and another gives the sign for them to run across the street. First Dunja, and then Aunt. An unmown meadow separates them from Ilonka's yard. They crawl through tall grass, which is sharp and dry. It smells sweet, like hay. Aunt pounds on the door.

'Ilonka, come out!'

Dunja thinks that this is the first time she's ever been to their front door. Ilonka and Karlo come out of the wardrobe. She opens the front door, holding him by the hand. He resists, he's big and strong. She can barely manage him. More women and children arrive in the yard. They flee through Ilonka's cornfield towards the train tracks, the fields and the Bosna. Stalks break under the weight of their bodies. Ilonka lags behind with Karlo. He's resisting and digging in his heels like Bekan did in the swamp when we were leaving the village. She yells at him that we're all going to be killed. He screams even louder.

The ballast on the train tracks crumbles beneath their feet. The tracks always smell the same, melted tar, hot metal, old wood. A bullet whizzes past Dunja's head and singes her hair. A whole lock of hair comes away in her hand. They descend from the tracks into the fields and run towards the Bosna. Dunja can't hear Karlo's screams any more, or the drumming of bullets, or her mother's voice. Just the roar of the river.

Dunja takes off her shoes on the riverbank. She wades in and the water submerges her ankles. It's as cold in summer as it is in the autumn. It's deeper and deeper; it's already up to her waist. Aunt holds her by the hand. The river is swift; it easily catches a child's light body in its current.

Rocks, sludge and slippery river grass under their feet. Fat carp that have overindulged on plastic and the flesh of carrion swim around them.

SILENCE

Darkness descends on the village across the Bosna. Women and children have gathered in front of the house with the weeping willow. They're silent and gaze at the forest in flame. Their wet feet are scratched and dirty. Dunja is sitting in the grass next to Bekan and patting him. If it wasn't covered by darkness, you would see that her face is not green any more but white, and her lips are pursed as if she has just eaten an unripe apple.

The first thing they hear is Grandmother's screams. She's hurrying down the narrow road, rolling like a black skein of yarn. Her arms stick out of it like two knitting needles. They sit her down on the concrete stairs in front of the house. Aunt brings her water and sugar. Grandmother wheezes, but a parched throat, like dust, won't take any water.

My brother and grandfather turn up at the gate.

Their silence is louder than Grandmother's wheezing.

NIGHT

Don't hesitate! Come in, please...

The house with the weeping willow is not locked.

Against whom should it be locked? Against thieves and criminals?

Follow me, but just be careful not to trip over some of the motionless bodies in the dark. They're everywhere, on sofas, beds, the floor. There's not enough room for them all. If you could only see them, you would be frightened by their eyes. They're wide open. Stuck. It wouldn't even help to pull them by the eyelashes. They would suffocate if their mouths weren't open. Hot smoke and silenced screams billow from them. For a second, tears constrict their throats, and the smoke stops, they cough and then it billows from them even more, like through a cleaned flue. It's stifling in the house. Why doesn't anybody open the windows?

The thick, frosted windowpane on the bathroom door has turned yellow.

The splashing of water can be heard.

My brother has locked himself in there. He's been standing in the bathtub for a long time, his face turned towards the mirror. His face is a black, quivering shadow in the oil lamp's flickering flame. He can't see the colour of his skin, but he can feel it beneath his fingers. Hardened blood tightens the skin like a fresh scar. It dissolves under the cold water. A mixture of our blood runs down his body and vanishes down the rusty drain in the bathtub. It smells like the barren soil around the mineral water spring.

In the dark, he can't see that he hasn't washed all the blood off and that it has been soaked up by the scratches on his white skin. He throws the towel he wiped himself with on the floor and stands on it. The clothes he puts on are someone else's and are too big. He shrinks in them.

My brother's tracksuit and trainers are in a plastic basin next to the bathtub. Aunt will burn them in the morning, behind the house where they burn the rubbish. It will stink of plastic and rotten meat.

Even though the well water has cooled his skin, hot currents continue to circulate under it. His heart pounds like that of a child mesmerised by a muddy river eddy, like the newborn mice from the house with its eyes gouged out. He lies down on the sofa in the kitchen. He stares at the darkness around him. He thinks he can hear a polecat, as big as a rabbit, twitching behind him, and he can hear its paws tapping on the linoleum. He doesn't know where to turn. The house is getting smaller; none of the windows can open. He would yell, but his mouth is full of dirt. His eyes are full of it. He can hear the shovel digging into the heap of grainy soil, which scatters into dust. I lie down next to my brother and squeeze his hand.

We can hear Mother speaking.

'Think of something nice, you'll fall asleep more easily.'

We think of the seaside. There's nothing more beautiful than the seaside. The air is salty and the pines smell good.

We're driving in the lorry with Father. Mother isn't going with us.

'I can't swim anyway.'

The ripped seats bob up and down and squeak. It's hot and dusty. We vomit into black nylon.

'Just a bit longer,' Father says. 'Just a bit longer.'

The salty air is abuzz with cicadas. Coconut suncream, pink ice creams. There's no end to the blueness.

We float and forget.

'Think of something nice,' Mother whispers.

IV

THE LAST PHOTOGRAPH

Let me show you our yard. Grandfather's already there. He's emerging from the cellar with his shirt unbuttoned and his sleeves rolled up. He stops next to the tap; he takes off his shirt and hangs it on the same nail that his crusty towel hangs from. The sun is just as strong today, so we won't miss a thing: only Grandfather's face has darkened as if his eyebrows have cast a shadow on it, as thick and cold as the forest shade. He pushes the wheelbarrow out of the shed and drops a shovel into it. He turns here and there, not knowing where to begin. The yard is a kicked naked body, all bruised and bloody. The dirt track is cold, dark-red gruel, a blood-pudding mixture. In winter, Grandfather lures the pig with crab apples, but it knows, it squeals and digs its trotters in. Grandfather first pats it and coos to it and then, when his trickery fails, gods and saints tumble out of his mouth. He leashes it with a cable and leads it out, then hits it with a hammer in the middle of the forehead. The pig can then only sob quietly, like Grandmother at the well. Grandfather sticks a knife into its neck, and Grandmother slides the rusty pan underneath to collect all the blood. The head and the slippery innards are put into the cauldron with boiling water. Later, Grandmother stuffs everything into the big meat grinder. She pours the blood over the gruel and then fills up the washed intestines.

'Eat! Go on, eat! They'll go off soon.'

Grandfather fills the wheelbarrow with the curdled blood from the track which has mixed with the dust and pebbles. There's already a big pile in the wheelbarrow, and it seems to Grandfather that he has only just started. He's drenched from the effort and the heat. as if his head is going to burst. He has disturbed a swarm of blowflies, which are now buzzing around him and sticking to droplets of sweat on his body. Grandfather raises his eyes towards the sky and screams like an animal. He throws the shovel by the road and takes the wheelbarrow to the swamp to empty it into the hole where all dead things are thrown.

Cover your nose with clean rags! Breathe through the mouth!

Although the sun rose ages ago, I'm still in the dark. The improvised morgue has no windows; it was a garage once. The shelves with tools were taken down from the walls. Bare concrete everywhere, nylon sheets spread out on the floor. We're lined up in three rows. I'm lying in the second, somewhere in the middle, wrapped up in rustling foil. It's silver on the inside and gold on the outside, like the smooth quilt fabric in Great-Aunt's room, the gold tin with maggot-infested luncheon meat. This is my evening gown. The shining of the foil in the dark reminds me of the tiny fireflies on that warm evening we arrived in the village across the Bosna.

The garage door is metal and can be raised like the bed in Mother's room. The light has eaten up all the darkness, but the cutting stench of stagnant death is unchanging. The photographer coughs and puts his sleeve to his nose. The foil rustles. He uncovers my bluish face and skinny body. Blue eyes, as unmoving as Julija's, beneath the slightly parted lids. The mouth has remained open like in the photograph taken on the roof of the red Lada. A thick stream of black blood has hardened under my nose. My hair is still beautiful, white, sun-soaked camomile flowers. There is a crown of purple crooked fingers above my head.

The photographer moves closer and uses his sleeve to wipe away a mixture of sweat and tears. He catches me through the lens and focuses. He takes my last photograph with just a click. In contrast to my father's Polaroid photograph, this one is clear, with all the details. My brother and father are standing in front of the garage. They're waiting for the photographer to come out. You can't speak through constricted throats. Their eyes have run dry.

Grandfather takes the cover off the well and puts it on the grass. He can't see his reflection on the water's surface; the water is just as black. Inside there is nothing but muffled silence and stillness. He throws in the pail. Stone, water, metal. He pours the water into the large bucket from the barn and rinses the concrete in front of our house. The water goes pink from the blood of the soldier with the black sash and runs into the dried grass, where the overturned black cauldron and the remains of the tomato sauce lie. The blowflies don't leave Grandfather alone – he waves his bear's paw in front of his face in vain.

The door to our house has stood open all night.

Be careful not to step on the glass; the windows have been shattered.

The rug has slipped off the wooden stairs. The creak can't be heard any more. A few more stairs and we're at the top, in the empty room drowned in concrete dust. If you drop to the floor and look closely, you'll see traces of bare feet in the dust and the large prints of black boots.

If I exhale, they'll disappear.

Here are my shoes, under the window.

Don't say anything! Here the quietest sounds are transformed into echoes.

The forest, the road and the long clothesline in the field above the house can be seen from the big windows. Smoke still rises from black holes in the forest, and the curtains on the clothesline have been transformed into blackened rags. You couldn't even make a bride's veil from them.

The silence from the well would prevail in the house if the doves weren't cooing under the eaves.

Let's go down now to the threshold! Sivka is sitting there, her nose red.

She has eaten the trampled asters in front of Grandmother's house.

FUNERAL

Although the dirt track has been scraped to the bone and the concrete washed down, the air still smells of iron. It's disseminated by the overstuffed blowflies, their bodies swollen to the point of bursting. They crash into each other in the air, they descend onto the pink puddles and rotten plums in the grass.

My brother is kneeling by the road and pulling up yellow marigolds from our flowerbed. The tough stems leave a strong green smell on his hands. Dry soil has embedded itself deep under his broken nails. He can't wash it out. The bouquet of marigolds is a burning sun. His skin is scratched underneath his T-shirt like scribbled white paper. It's not visible, but it's soaked in other people's blood; skin as white as cotton soaks up everything you spill on it. He's standing alone in the middle of the road. The razed landscape in his irises, weak coils of smoke rising.

He can't smell the sun in his hands.

Warm clouds of mist emanate from Father's mouth. He's sitting in the shade, on the stairs outside the wide-open front door. He's watching the concrete dry and the heat evaporating from it. Sweat is dripping from his bald head. Colder than fear. Cigarette butts trampled by a ribbed sole.

Father also wears tightly laced black boots.

Grandfather is standing with his back turned to Father. There is a bucket full of water in the concrete trough. He scoops the water with his hand and splashes it behind his neck, down his back, under the armpits. The water runs down his skin and is soaked up by the camouflage trousers. Grandfather doesn't even seem to notice it. He washes his face and runs wet hands through his thick hair. He wipes himself down with his crusty towel. He can't even smell it; he's used to it, just like he's used to his bear's paw. He puts on his shirt and buttons it up.

They say nothing. They pass by the silver birches, the barbed wire and the roses of which only the thorny stems remain, between two large pines, and turn left towards Spasoje's house, towards the spring and the cemetery. They walk slowly, following the winding road. Single file. My brother goes first, the sun in his hands gazing at the ground.

The houses are quiet. Some yards are open, rubber sandals and leather shoes strewn in front of doors. White plastic buckets and baskets full of half-rotten fruit. The gate to Spasoje's yard is closed. He spent all day and night yesterday in the hayloft. He came out at dawn when everything fell quiet. He's standing in his yard and watching the road. He nods by way of a greeting. He takes off his hat and stands by the gate. He watches them disappear around a curve. He crosses himself.

The elderberry blossoms next to the hayloft have turned into juicy black berries.

The cemetery is on the hill. You can see it clearly from the forest. That's why the grave was dug at the foot of the cemetery, in the shade of tall oak trees. The sun never reaches the spot.

It was dug by the soldiers with pickaxes. There is no difference between digging trenches and digging graves. Their boots are muddy because the soil is so damp there. Water floods in from everywhere.

They brought me in an old white van. Thick ropes attached to the heavy wooden coffin. They carry me on their shoulders. Grandfather, Uncle, Father and my brother. My uncle came with the van driver. The coffin is light, but the weight of the clear sky has fallen on their broad shoulders.

The priest's arms are spread wide, white wings, his skin soft and clean, smelling of soap. On both sides of him, there are exhausted legs, shaky knees and muddy boots. The priest's voice is even and soft. The coffin falls into the muddy swamp. The sound is disquieting, like a hammer blow to a nail's head. The muddy ropes have been removed and rolled into a coiled snake. The clods of earth are cold in the hand, like the chill in Grandmother's lilacs. The clods hit the lid of the coffin. Dirty fingers are wiped on trousers. Male grief is mute.

My brother puts the sunny marigolds down under the cross with my name on it. The yellow wax of Mother's prayer candle drips on the ground.

HOSPITAL

Sugar almonds rustle in Dunja's pocket. They're wrapped in clear cellophane. They arrived from Caritas in a packet with rice, sugar, tins, soap and toothbrushes. They got them in the city of B—. Mother is in hospital there. My father and brother are visiting her.

They stand in the doorway of room 7. The beds have been pushed next to each other. Motionless bodies, like those on the nylon in the garage. They're covered in white paper as thin and soft as a paper napkin. Metal rods peek out of Mother's leg. It's raised high. They can see the black skin and green nails and smell the stench of the butcher's shop, of the morgue. It's hot. Oppressive heat in the open window.

They hesitate at the door. Mother looks at them without saying a word. They approach slowly. My brother seems skinnier and younger to her. He has become so much smaller that she could take him in her arms. Father clutches her sweaty hand.

'Have you buried her?'

A nod. Her body convulses. Tears stream down her cheeks. Her greying hair soaks them up.

✳

Dunja is melting from sugar and almonds. She descends the road towards the riverbank. There's ever more rubbish there. How can the world still be the same? She wonders about the faces at the gates at dusk, the birds above the fields. Only the sky has changed. Clouds are gathering on the edges of the forest and over it, like the froth on the sides of a pail of freshly milked milk. The days have grown shorter. The sky quickly turns to grey and descends over the Bosna. She sits on the cold pebbles. The Bosna flows swiftly when you get closer. Dunja can still hear the roar. A bike turns onto the bank and brakes suddenly. Pebbles scatter. Goran throws his bike down and sits next to Dunja.

'Were you there too? Did they really kill her?'

He speaks quietly, but his voice echoes in Dunja's ears.

She starts crying. Goran sits quietly and looks at the river. Dunja takes a sweet out of her pocket and lowers it into his hand. The sound of pebbles underfoot. The road is long. She can hear her blood pulsing through her veins, her heart pounding.

She calms down under the weeping willow. In the dark.

THE THUMBLING

Dunja and my uncle are standing in the corridor of the hospital in front of a white, flaking door. It stinks of bleach like the school toilet. The toilets in hospitals and schools are rusty squatting ones. The cisterns are placed too high, and you have to stand on tiptoe to reach the black cord and flush. After, the cisterns gurgle for a long time. There are two narrow glass panes on the door. Dunja looks at the sluggish female bodies through them, their backs hunched, faces grey. Their hands rest on their deflated bellies, and they clutch large pieces of cotton soaked in black blood between their legs. The cotton can't soak up the clots, so the clots remain stuck to the surface. They're dark and smooth like chicken livers. In the toilets, women stand over the squatting toilets because they've just been stitched up between the legs.

Dunja doesn't recognise her mother. Her skin is blotchy, her mouth collapsed. No green crayon on her eyes. They're red from crying. Her nightie is short and loose, with large slits at the front and back. Look at her small white breasts with their black, swollen nipples. Her belly is thin, with thick black hairs beneath. Her mother is completely different. Her palms sweat, her body cramps and shrinks at the thought of such a mother.

Where can you escape from your mother?

Hospital noises cut the air. The echo of female voices and the crying of newborn babies mix with the clinking of scissors and metal pans. Dunja wrings her sweaty hands with fear.

When thumb-sized babies are born, they are not buried. They pulse out of the womb together with blood. Like when the skin on a tomato breaks, and then the juice and seed spill. The juice from the womb ends up in metal pans. Everything is thrown out, but nobody knows where. The pans are as cold as the scissors.

Aunt's belly never got to grow.

The baby was a thumbling.

TRAINERS

The summer is at an end.

That's clear from the smell of the stagnant, damp air. It seems that the plants in the gardens have been completely dried up by the strong sun and there is nothing but dust in the blackened fruit. Nevertheless, if you take a stem and snap it, you'll see that it's still moist inside and that there is black juice in the fruit. It will run down your fingers like ink.

You simultaneously dry up and rot.

Here are the clouds too! They're grey and far away but they're moving swiftly. When they descend on us, they will be completely black. A heavy, cold rain will descend from them, and the earth will swallow up all the rot.

Dunja observes the oncoming clouds from the window of her room in the house with the weeping willow. They seem unstoppable and violent. A wind starts blowing out of the blue and it raises the white hairs on her arms. She looks across the Bosna, to the village and the forest. She hears the yellowed cattails rustling and their flakes, as soft as dandelion clocks, are scattered by the wind. The toads croak ever louder, sensing the storm.

She's still wearing shorts and a vest, even though it's cooler. She comes down the stairs, and instead of flip-flops she puts on her old black shoes, the ones she carried in her hands when she was crossing the Bosna. They're still beautiful, with straps on the side, the leather is still good; there's only a small hole on the left shoe, above the big toe. They're small for her, so she keeps her toes curled. She can hear her mother clanging with the pots in the kitchen and rubber slides squeaking on the linoleum. They're alone in the house with the weeping willow; the other families have already returned to our village. Aunt is still afraid; she'll stay till winter. Since she's come back from the hospital, she's ever thinner, and the button on her skirt can't be moved any further. Grandmother bakes bread for her, brings her butter and milk for breakfast. She eats less than Dunja. Uncle drops in sometimes at night. Dunja leaves the house without telling her where she's going. Bekan is lying in a field tied to a stake. She kneels down and kisses him between his tiny horns. She descends to the road and hurries on.

Only my father and grandmother remain in the house with the gouged-out eyes. My brother has been sent to my mother. They have transferred her to Z—. Friends of Mother's who live there will take care of him. Father sits at the table smoking. Grandmother is at the stove. Lard is sizzling in the pan. Grandmother seasons the pie in the pan with it. All the doors in the house are open, but no fresh air makes it inside. The smell is always the same, damp and rotting wood. The steam in the kitchen has been soaked up by the walls and the sticky curtains. Grandmother's sweating. It's running down her cheeks. She tightens the knot on her headscarf and sits down. Her body spills over the stool.

Sivka's teeth are red. She's standing on the threshold meowing. A dead mouse lies in front of her. Grandmother gets up and waves the broom. She sweeps the mouse onto the dustpan and throws it onto the grass in front of the house. It lies on the grass with its eyes open. Several large drops of rain hit the blue Salonit tiles over the veranda. Grandmother sees Dunja running towards her.

Dunja takes off her shoes in the hallway. Her feet are cold and bare. The dust from the dirty floor sticks to her feet. My trainers were left leaning against the wall. Nobody has touched them. Flies have dotted them black and an airy spider web has covered them. In the kitchen, Dunja greets them quietly. Grandmother remains in the hallway and presses the sole of Dunja's shoe to the sole of my trainer.

On the table there's no tablecloth. A pan sits in the middle of it. Traces of dried water and greasy fingers on plates. Grandmother cuts the pie and takes the pieces out with her hands and places them on the plates.

Dunja feels nauseous. From the smell of the house and the grease in the pie.

'Eat something. Look how thin you are. Your legs'll snap beneath you.'

Grandmother swallows large pieces of pie.

'Her shoes are worn through.'

Dunja's throat constricts, the bite gets stuck.

Tears spill onto the table.

'She can take the trainers,' my father says.

'We're eating now. No crying.'

Nylon bags rustle in the hallway. Dunja is standing on the veranda. The rain is pouring down harder.

Grandmother throws the trainers into a nylon bag. A small mouse wriggles out of one. It scratches the bag, panicked. Dunja starts crying and runs off down the street. The rain and cold wind whip her face. Grandmother stands on the veranda with the bag in her hand. She watches Dunja's swinging hair until it disappears behind the hedge.

BEKAN

A lambskin is now spread out next to Dunja's bed. When she gets up in the morning, her bare feet step onto knotted, curly fur. She tried to comb it out, but she broke the comb's teeth on the tougher knots. It's gone grey from the dust and rot. Grandfather used to have it nailed to the wooden door of the granary, above the tap. He had turned the inside towards the sun, which hardened and became as rough as the skin of a fox that bites its own tail around a female's neck. Grandfather rubbed ash into the leather; his bear's paw turned completely grey. After that, he poured coarse salt over the leather. Blowflies flee from it.

Bekan broke free from the stake and ran onto the road through the open gate. The car that hit him didn't even stop; it slowed just for a second and then disappeared round the bend in a yellow cloud of dust and smoke. Bekan was lying by the road next to the canal, his legs broken. Bleating quietly. The rope still hanging around his neck.

Uncle slaughtered him. Dunja couldn't watch. She fled to her room in the attic and closed the window. She's lying on her bed, breathless, like when you fall on your back on the ice, and you can't catch your breath. Uncle hangs Bekan on the bleeding hook by the back feet and skins him. His fur is still clean, with just a bit of dried blood under the neck. The knife penetrates the stomach and splits it. The innards drop into a plastic bucket. Without his skin, Bekan is thin and transparent, like Dunja. His flesh is bruised.

Dunja's whole body is shaking. Her pillowcase is completely wet. She doesn't leave the attic till dusk. She opens the window. Nobody is in the yard. Just the big bleeding hook and the buckets, rinsed out with well water. A cold wind hits her face. She closes her eyes.

The house with the weeping willow smells of meat. Aunt is roasting it in a large pan. The bread dipped in grease is soft. It doesn't smell of yeast. Dunja eats too.

TANTRUM

The fogs have become thicker. The branches in the orchards are wet and black. Tiny droplets of dew glisten on large spider webs. All that remains of the rotted plums in the grass are black pips and some dried flesh. It's been drizzling since dawn. Grandfather is lying on the sofa and scratching his bony feet on the sofa's wooden armrest. He has been sleeping in the same clothes – camouflage trousers and a khaki jumper – for days. He wakes up and throws off the old blanket. It stinks of dust and mould, of rakija. He gets up in the half-dark and pats down his trouser pockets. He takes out a matchbox and lights the wick on the oil lamp. Quick smoke flows. It hits the low ceiling and transforms it into a black cotton wool sky. It descends on Grandfather's head.

There's a glass bottle next to the bed, with just a couple of sips of rakija left in it. Grandfather downs it in one and growls with satisfaction. It's cold in the cellar, but Grandfather is sweating. Cold drops trickle down the deep furrows of his forehead, gathering in his thick brows. His temples throb. He puts on his boots. They've shaped themselves around his wide feet. He starts tightening the laces. A drop of sweat from his forehead trickles to the tip of his nose. He feels its weight, his eyes cloud over. He pulls the laces. They snap. The drop from his nose hits the floor. The cellar roars. Grandfather's shadow grows on the wall. It's gigantic. A scream escapes from his chest. He kicks the bottles lined up next to the display cabinet. Glass flashes in the dark like lightning in the early evening hours. Shards lie scattered on the floor. Grandfather sees his reflection in the mirror. It's black and cracked.

He takes scissors and a length of old cord from a drawer. He threads it through instead of the laces. His soles grind the glass. He puts on his jacket and places his rifle on his shoulder. He blows out the oil lamp and leaves. He pays no attention to the deserted yards. He can hear the babble of the mineral water fountains. All that remains of the old tavern on the hill is a bullet-riddled ruin among the shrubs and the upright burdock. The raindrops are colder and sharper.

He stops next to a low building with a flat roof. The front has metal bars and a padlock. The glass beneath is taped together with stickers and ads for ice cream and detergent. In the half-light, stacked cartons are visible. A guard stands outside, smoking. They know each other well. As soon as he sees Grandfather, he goes to the storehouse and unlocks it. He shouts and two captive soldiers in dirty uniforms and rubber boots come out of the storehouse, carrying poleaxes. They head towards the forest. Grandfather follows them, as he does every day. The forest is damp, full of black mushrooms and soft grass. The leaves rustle above. The cold rain runs down their necks. A green woodpecker flies past and screeches twice.

The trench is long and muddy. Bodies stick out of it. Arms rise and fall. Clods of damp soil scatter through the air. The two soldiers descend into the trench, and Grandfather sits down at a wooden table. A grey old soldier sees him. He takes a bottle and glasses out of his bag. He pours rakija into them. Glasses clink. Throats warm up.

He takes them back to the storehouse in the afternoon. The door is open. The muddy poleaxes in front look like dried flowers sprouting from the concrete. Their footsteps are slow; their boots heavier from the mud. Grandfather doesn't hear anything; he just sees them opening their mouths. He turns round and heads towards the village school. The army canteen is there now.

The road to the school is steep. Rivulets of dirty water and pebbles run down it. Large oak trees line both sides. Long tables are set up under asbestos sheets in front of the school. The women mix boiling and cold water to wash the dishes. Plates are piled high, clanging heaps of spoons and forks. Their sleeves are rolled up.

They unload the tall military pot of beans and sliced bread from the army vehicle. They stand in a queue in the hall. Two classrooms in the school have been adapted for dining. Grandfather is standing there in his wet jacket; he doesn't remove his rifle from his shoulder. The queue moves forwards slowly, and Milo, the head of the canteen, is standing behind the big table. A taut apron stretches over his paunch, a ladle in his hand. He takes two scoops from the military pot and puts them in a plate.

'Still doing women's work,' Grandfather says.

Milo's mouth stretches into a smile. His tongue seems like a large, slimy snail to Grandfather. He can't look at his bulging eyes. If he strained himself they would burst or fall out and roll on the floor. He puts the beans onto Grandfather's plate. Grandfather takes a seat and puts the rifle down next to him, by the window. He eats greedily. His mouth is a machine. The classroom reverberates with laughter, the clattering of dishes and spoons.

Grandfather eats everything up and throws the plate down in front of Milo.

'Any seconds?'

'None!' Milo's mouth stretches.

Red blotches appear on Milo's face. He turns his back to Grandfather and loudly closes the lid on the military pot.

'Fill it up! I'll kill you like a wild animal!' Grandfather yells.

Laughter and droplets of saliva spill out of Milo's mouth.

The furrows on Grandfather's face become streams. The murmur in his ears becomes an unbearable noise. He grabs his rifle and shoots. The first bullet goes through Milo's head as if it were pudding. He riddles his whole body with bullets. Blood flows like red wine from a pierced barrel.

Grandmother never unties the knot on her headscarf any more.

RETURN

The snow in the yard of the house with the weeping willow is trampled. Beneath the whiteness, mud. Dunja and Aunt throw their suitcases and plastic bags into the trunk. Everyone has already returned to the village. Aunt is in a loose blue coat with a high collar and large buttons. Underneath it, instead of a muffler, she wears a headscarf with large bronze flowers. Dunja wraps the flowers around herself. They smell of perfume, of hyacinths. Aunt's face is visible in the rear-view mirror. Her skin red, green crayon in the corners of her eyes. The engine grates but still catches right away. A yellow book with a charred cover and a black book with cake recipes are in the bag next to Dunja. She's in a black jacket made of rough baize, which makes her even paler and skinnier. The car drives out of the gate onto the road and disappears around the bend. The weeping willow with its long frozen branches stands in the abandoned yard. The house is now empty. Its darkness yearns, motionless and silent. It falls on the old wood, the dusty fabric and lace hanging over the window. Things go cold from it, they forget touch. They rust and rot from desire.

The house with the gouged-out eyes is even uglier in the snow. The black pits even darker. The windowpanes on the ground floor are fogged up. Grandmother is standing on the veranda in a dress and black coat. The black headscarf is tied behind her head. Grandmother hasn't stopped crying since the summer and has been crying even more since Grandfather went to prison. She's ashamed to go out among other people. Aunt gets out and takes her bags to the car. There's no more room in the trunk so she puts them on the back seat next to Dunja. Grandmother gets into the front seat with difficulty. She turns round and looks at Dunja. She wipes her tears. All are silent. The smell of the house with the gouged-out eyes emanates from Grandmother's body.

They don't go home via the road through the fields but take the main road through town. The streets are black fire pits, the asphalt is riddled with big potholes, dirty lakes. Sheets of nylon on the windows of the buildings instead of glass. On the blue bridge, Dunja looks at the swollen Bosna. It is taking away the rubbish, dry branches and dead animals. The roar is audible even though the windows are shut. It's always in her ear.

Our yard is completely white, without any human tracks. The car descends the road and stops between our house and Grandmother's. Grandmother covers her face with her hands. She's shaking from crying. Aunt gets out and takes the suitcases and bags, which she leaves in front of the cellar. Grandmother remains standing next to the well.

HEAVEN

Sunbeams in the frozen canopy of the crab apple tree. Tiny crystals flash white, green and purple. Pure mother-of-pearl. The air is still. All that stirs are Spasoje's last breaths escaping from his mouth and dissipating into warm smoke. He's lying underneath the crab apple tree with his eyes open. It seems to him that he's just stuck to the dry branches under the snow. Beneath him is ice, frozen ground. All smells fade in the winter. They become an empty sharpness, but Spasoje can smell basil, the gentleness of skin like milk that has gone sour.

'Fool! Fool!'

The wind blows and the branches spill silver dust over him. Spasoje knows he's in heaven.

That's how you die in winter. Silently and unnoticed.

It's getting dark. The cow in Spasoje's barn is mooing from hunger. She's going crazy. Not even a willow switch would help.

A cold wind blows down from the mountain and whimpers among the walls of the oldest house in the village.

TANK

Ilonka and Karlo are trying in vain to light a fire in the stove. The walls of the house are icy. The fire devours the firewood, the walls the heat. Grandmother says that a house is like a man: once ice gets into its bones, it's hard to get it out. Ilonka's plastic Christmas tree, decorated with silver baubles and moulted shiny tinsel, stands in the corner near the sofa. Instead of snow spray, Karlo has put balls of cotton wool on the tips of the branches. There are no lights; there's no electricity anyway. They put on coats and woollen socks in their leather shoes. Ilonka has a plastic jug in her hand. It's gone yellow from the mineral water. It smells flavourless.

The footpath along the road is narrow. Ilonka seeks Karlo's hand. He's hidden it in his pocket. He's too big for this. In the other one, he is carrying the full jug. It snows even harder. Snow and sleet. Ilonka doesn't hear the tank behind her. The tied headscarf presses on her ears. She's caught by the right caterpillar track and run over. Karlo rolls away into the stream and stops at the metal fence which protects the yard from the road. The tank slows down and stops. A soldier emerges from the narrow opening. He mutely regards the boy yelling in the stream. People rush out of the houses. They're all yelling at once. The soldier doesn't understand a single word of what the people on the road are saying. Karlo flails his arms and legs in the muddy water.

'Mummy! Mummy!'

Karlo can't remain at home alone. They take him to his cousins.

The smoke has stopped coming out of Ilonka's chimney. The air gets darker. A shadow has fallen over everything; only the Christmas tree and small silver baubles twinkle in the corner.

CAKES

In winter, the apple tree branches are glassy and frozen apples hang from their tips. The winter and north wind have saved them from rot and bird beaks. Dunja is tiny beneath the big canopy. Black baize and brown velvet hang from her skinny body. They say scarecrows look like this in the fields.

The snow is trampled and muddy. Flakes fall on her golden hair and melt there. This is how raindrops drip along the long corn leaves.

Grandfather's rakes are leaning against the barn wall. Dunja takes one, the longest. It's curved and cold. She can barely handle it. She hits the thin branches, and the fruit and tips of the branches fall onto the dirty snow. They break easily. The frozen apples are like stones. They emanate no freshness or ripe aroma. Blotches and tiny wrinkles have appeared on the apples just like on her mother's face. She undoes her jacket, lifts the hem of her sweater and throws the apples into it like into a basket. The rake is left under the apple tree. Dunja runs off down the road.

She places the apples on a tray and leaves them next to the stove to thaw more quickly. Yellow liquid seeps from them, and the fruit get smaller and more wrinkled. They're soft to the touch and don't smell. The walnuts are tiny, black. Dunja hits them with a split log on the large chopping board. She puts the shelled nuts in a plastic bowl. Her mother mixes the eggs. A black book with a recipe for apple and almond cake lies open on the table. They don't have most of the ingredients, but they make a sponge cake with grated apples and walnuts. Only when the batter has risen in the tray in the oven does the aroma of apples and sugar become noticeable.

There are still no curtains on the big window. The cake in Dunja's hand is warm. She can't wait for it to cool. She's standing there watching Grandmother's house and our house. Smoke can be seen from Grandmother's chimney. Ours is deserted. Father rarely drops by. There are grey houses and muddy yards above the road, in thick smoke. Erect pine trees dusted with snow. The black burnt spots are still visible. Great big fire pits. Snowflakes disappear there without a trace.

IF YOU DREAM
OF THE DEAD

I try to wake her up in vain. You know how soundly children sleep. My hands are as cold as the darkness in the room; she can't feel them on her hot face, just like she can't feel the summer she is dreaming of.

Black ink has seeped from the hole with the dead animals into the swamp. The thick black mass reaches our knees. Our legs are herons' legs. We can barely lift them out of the sticky silt full of bones, ribs, knees and skulls.

My white dress is already dirty.

I stand in front of Dunja, her arms extended towards me, but she can't catch me. Another step or two and we'll meet on the train tracks. It's dry there, wood, rock, iron. Black water trickles down our legs onto the tracks. Dunja lifts her gaze towards the sun. It's as big as the sky.

The hedge along the train track swells before our eyes. Blackberries grow as big as a clenched fist. They can barely fit in our mouths. They burst and splatter in a sticky redness that runs down our chins. Swarms of blowflies rise from the swamp. There are more and more of them. Any longer and we won't be able to see the sky.

I'm far away. Dunja turns round, wanting to run towards me, but she can't move her feet. The ballast is starting to crumble, the tracks tremble. The sound of the engine behind me. The train comes ever closer. She lifts her arms high; she looks like a scarecrow in the cornfield.

I smile at her.

The train has already rumbled past.

Dunja opens her eyes and grabs at the darkness with her hands. She pulls the quilt over her head.

'If you dream of the dead, pray for them,' Grandmother says.

Dunja falls asleep just before dawn after an infinite number of Our Fathers.

DARKNESS

Dunja feels she could touch the clouds if she stood on tiptoe. She doesn't know if the sky is black in itself or from the coal smoke which eddies from the boiling-hot chimneys. In winter, the village is found squashed between the icy bog on the ground and the carbon darkness that descends over the roofs. Winter's hold doesn't let up until spring and only then, when the sun shines, does all the misery of the small yards and neglected houses become evident.

In front of the door to the cellar are Grandmother's galoshes and Grandfather's boots. They let him out of jail for the weekend. Dunja hasn't seen him since the summer. She sees the yellow light of the oil lantern through the misty pane on the door. Grandmother keeps it lit all day because the cellar is in total darkness during winter. Dunja notices that only the silver birches along the path are beautiful and festive, as if they didn't belong in this place and as if the rain, snow and sun couldn't harm them in any way. Dunja's hands are bare, wet and cold, and so the touch of the needles is more painful. She pulls her sleeves over her hands and tries to break off a birch branch. She doesn't succeed.

'You have to use shears.'

Dunja shudders at the sound of Grandfather's voice. She stops and then turns slightly. She doesn't recognise him; he's further away than he has ever been. The thick, dishevelled hair is no more. It is short and spiky now. His forehead is high and bony, his eyes sparkling. There's a large bruise across his face. She wonders if Grandfather has a rifle behind his back. Grandfather leaves and brings shears from the shed. He cuts branches and places them in Dunja's arms, as if she were carrying a baby or an armload of firewood. She can't smell rakija on Grandfather any more: just soot and garlic.

'Is that enough?'

Dunja says nothing, just nods imperceptibly. She looks at Grandfather once more and runs home as fast as she can. Squelching beneath her boots. Sprays of mud from the path splatter her back and hair. She takes the branches into the house and throws them onto the floor. She can see Grandfather standing in the middle of the road looking towards their house. She moves away from the window, but she can still feel Grandfather's sparkling eyes watching her.

From the small white Sarabon suitcase, in which she once got a New Year's present, she takes out some Christmas baubles and silver tinsel that Grandmother calls angel hair. She ties the silver birches into a bouquet and decorates them with baubles, showering them with the shiny tinsel.

The snow is falling ever harder, the flakes are large and heavy. The black baize is getting heavier, the long hair darkens from the moisture. Grandmother comes out of the privy and shouts:

'Where do you think you're going bareheaded?'

Dunja says she'll be back straight away and runs out onto the road. Grandmother dismisses her with a wave of her hand. There's no snow on the road; the snowflakes have melted on the wet asphalt and in the deep potholes full of dirty water. Sweaters, greying sheets, torn cotton nappies and kitchen towels are stretched out on clotheslines in the trampled yards. People don't come out of their homes. Twig brooms, galoshes and leather shoes are strewn on the wet concrete in front of the doors.

The gate in the wooden fence around Spasoje's property is closed. The snow is untouched, disturbed only by the tracks of cats' paws and three-toed birds' claws. Dunja halts, hesitates briefly, but opens the gate and goes in. This is the first time that she has stepped onto his property. Her legs tremble; she is afraid that Spasoje's ghost might fly out of the house and kill her with his axe. She turns round and goes back to the road. A lorry drives past and splatters her with mud.

The ground at the foot of the cemetery is trampled. My grave looks like a piece of a cultivated field powdered with snow. Traces of hardened wax all over the place. Dunja puts down her bouquet of decorated silver birch branches and crosses herself. She takes a sugar almond wrapped in clear cellophane out of the pocket of her black jacket and places it under the cross.

The snow comes down harder. It metamorphoses into sleet. She can feel the drops coming down faster and sharper. They stab her cheeks and forehead. She closes her eyes.

Only the darkness is peaceful.

V

THE OLD PHOTOGRAPH

I come out of the cold darkness of Grandmother's cellar. Look at the air, shimmering gold! Has a hot wind lifted the dust from the road – or have white lilies dispersed their pollen here from somewhere? The sky is also cloudless today, cut by black cables with gatherings of motionless birds. High up above them, a white line is being drawn.

> Plane, plane, up so high,
> drop us sweets from the sky.

I follow Mother's muddy tracks. She's standing before the concrete trough with the tap. There's a bucket full of overripe tomatoes next to her. A jet of water splashes and hits the concrete, tiny droplets bouncing off it. They shimmer orange, yellow and purple. Mother washes her hands and splashes cold water on her face and the back of her neck. She takes off the galoshes, which have grown heavy from the mud, and puts on her flip-flops. Her legs are dusty to the knees, to the hem of her dress. When she walks, she drags her right leg and has to raise her toes so that her flip-flop doesn't slip off. The skin around the scars on her leg has wrinkled and darkened. If you put your finger on the marks, you can feel them, gentle and rough at the same time, like the flesh beneath the cap of a large forest mushroom. Wounds never heal anyway; they're just covered by thin skin. Be careful! They crack open at the gentlest touch.

The house still smells the same, the pantry of vanilla sugar and lemon.

Mother is standing by the kitchen window. She moves the curtain aside and the strong light hits her face. These days, the light is yellow and speckled even on sunny days. I place my hands on her. Can you feel her bones under the skin grown thin? She has shrunk and shrivelled like a forgotten apple. All juice has evaporated from her. Her hair has dimmed and has been cut very short. Dust more than two decades old emanates from her.

From the display cabinet with the crystal, she removes the photograph of the old Lada. She turns it towards the light and examines it as if to discover something that wasn't there the last time. The wall clock strikes five o'clock. A sun as large as an apple hits the back of Mother's head. She feels as if her legs will completely give way. My voice rings in her ears.

Mummy! Mummy!

A song as soft as a cat's paws on carpet.

Mother's eyes fill with bubbles of mineral water.

SCAR

We're sitting in the shade of the chestnut tree that stands below the forest. From here, from the slope, you have a good view of everything. The road, the houses, the fields and the train tracks. What fall into the grass from the treetops aren't baby squirrels but fruit which have ripened too early. The blackened, spiky membranes have cracked and dried up. The wild animals from the forest are becoming ever braver, emerging from the forest and eating the chestnuts.

There are no more crooked concrete stairs. They were pulled down and the ground was quickly overrun by grass and weeds. If you could break through the dense thicket, you would see that only the foundations of the tavern remain. Men now drink in the taverns in town after work. Dunja would say that when we grew up our village would become a town, because towns spread quickly. They cover the ground in concrete and build skyscrapers taller than the tops of the old chestnut trees. We would live on the highest floor, like in a film, and we would watch other people's windows. Lamps being put out before bedtime, curtains swaying in open windows, people sitting at their dining room tables and gesticulating with their hands, and newlyweds embracing before sleep.

We descend along the road. An ugly scar instead of the mineral water spring. Someone has covered the spring with concrete. It's overrun by milkweed, which has turned blue from exhaust fumes. Nevertheless, the water has had to break through somewhere, so the red soil around the scar bubbles. Boiling water in a rusty pan, green and warm along the edges. Be careful not to step in it!

The houses along both sides of the road are still abandoned. They've been for sale for a long time: the lettering and phone numbers sprayed on the façades in black paint have faded. The rusty gates can't be opened any more. They have become one with the ground for a while now. Nothing blooms around them any more, as if the plants were tired of blossoming in vain.

The wooden fence around Spasoje's property has completely rotted and gone green with moss. The gate stands wide open, but tall nettles bar entry to uninvited guests. It appears as if no one has set foot there for a long time. Everything else is how he left it. Strewn shoes, dirty bottles, a large tree stump and an axe on the veranda. Someone has padlocked the door, although the old windows have been shattered by bad weather and you can clearly see inside. The old rusty stove, the bed without a mattress and the blackened pillow. Water has penetrated everything: the walls, the wooden floor, the timber... Even mice don't drop by any more. Some roof tiles have slipped, and someone has mended the empty spaces with pieces of nylon. From afar, they look like small skylights. I don't know how many more storms it will weather. When it caves in, the wind and the damp will devour its walls, and the last clue that the village once looked completely different, that it smelled of dusty elderflowers and spring water, will disappear.

SUN

My grave is on a hill. They transferred it from the foot of the hill the year my mother returned to the village with my brother. They didn't leave the house that day. Mother knew where they would bury me and that the ground there was dry and bare. The grey hairs on Grandmother's head are thin blades of grass. She sits by the window and gazes at the forest. She never goes there. The sound of the pickaxe digging into the hard ground rings in her head. The earth crumbles beneath her fingers. Her fingers are yellow. Only earth can smell like that.

Father brought Mother and Brother back. An eight-hour trip on dusty back roads. Mother saw the two large pine trees from afar. The whole village was waiting for her along the road. The car turned onto our dirt track between the two pine trees. Mother covered her face with her hands. Father helped her get out of the car. She leant on crutches. Everyone was silent. Mother's tears flowed swiftly. Dunja stood behind Aunt. Mother hugged her. The crying became ever louder.

Brother was being treated with tablets. Three tablets daily silenced the noise. They cooled the back of his head and dropped darkness over his eyes. He forgot about the weight of my body in his embrace and the feel of my eyelids on the tips of his fingers.

There's a marble monument on my grave now. In the picture, I am big and smiling.

At my feet, Grandmother and Grandfather lie together.

Grandmother went cold even before her heart broke. Mother and Aunt pressed their palms to her forehead as if she were a sick child. Her skin went blue, her throat wheezed like when she sat on the stairs in front of the house with the weeping willow.

They dressed Grandmother in a nightgown and warm socks for her funeral. They tied a headscarf around her bald head. The knot behind her head was no longer pulled tight.

Grandfather didn't sober up after Grandmother's funeral. He hid the bottles in the display cabinet where Grandmother kept the coffee and sugar. Dunja would stand at the door of the cellar, watching Grandfather drink out of the bottle. He wouldn't let go of it until he had emptied it, as if it were a glass in his hand. They would find him lying on the woodpile, in front of the shed, in the barn. Calls from the village would let us know they'd found him in a canal or a muddy ditch. Father and Uncle would lift him up and lie him down on the sofa under the window. They would pour away the rakija and lock him in the cellar. Grandfather would open his eyes. He couldn't see Grandmother on the other sofa. He would beat at the locked door with his bear's paw. He would yell. He fled through the window, which looked out onto the road and the apple tree. There were no sandbags there any more. The phone on the stool rang in vain.

Father found him dead at the table. All the bottles next to him were empty.

His heart broke too.

Grandmother and Grandfather aren't smiling in the pictures on the marble monument.

My brother stands at the foot of my grave. He's tall and muscular. His hands are still pale. His fingers long.

He puts the sunny marigolds down on the monument.

I smile.

IN CONVERSATION WITH ANĐELKA RAGUŽ

- *In Late Summer* is the first novel you have translated into English. What was your relationship with the novel? What drew you to translate it?

In Late Summer was my first foray, and hopefully not the last, into literary translation, although I've been translating all kinds of texts, predominantly non-fiction and academic articles, since the 1990s. When I first started working at the University of Mostar, among my first generation of students was Magdalena Blažević, the author of *In Late Summer*. Twenty-odd years later, Magdalena approached me about translating her short-story collection, *Celebration*, and her first novel, *In Late Summer*. Magdalena's mastery in depicting vivid scenes from everyday life in Bosnia and Herzegovina with such economy enchanted me I recognised the uniqueness and excellence of her writing. and began to translate with a dose of trepidation.

- You moved from Australia to Bosnia and Herzegovina as an adult in 1990, two years before the Bosnian War began. What was it like to translate a book with a child's perspective of that period? How did your own memories influence your writing?

The child's innocent perspective, not just on the war but on everyday life and the relations of the people around her, simultaneously defamiliarizes the events described and partially distances the reader from the horrors. Its overall effect is poignant, heart-wrenching and horrifying, underlining the realisation that the innocent were the true victims of the war. During the translation process, I tried to detach myself emotionally as much as possible for the simple reason that I could not allow my experiences and opinions to intrude on the translation of the child's perspective. Unfortunately, nearly thirty years after the war, the trauma and memories are still fresh, and it comes as no surprise that many authors have written and still write about the war in Bosnia and Herzegovina.

- *In Late Summer* is a deeply moving novel. I wonder if you could tell us about your emotional connection to the work. How did you feel when you were translating it?

Naturally, the subject of war always evokes bitter memories: of friends and relatives who lost their lives, of friends who suffer from PTSD, of the lives destroyed by the war, of people who were forced to leave their homes, of the generations who lost their innocence. Ivana's death and its effect on her family and the effect of the war on the village itself in the novel are just a snippet of what transpired in Bosnia and Herzegovina during the war.

- *In Late Summer* is full of beautiful, often impressionistic images. Did you have any difficulty rendering these into English? What were your biggest challenges when translating the novel?

The images themselves were not so much of a challenge as they are unique to the narrator's sensibility and function on the level of literary symbols in the work. What resonated strongly with me was the way every image that is evoked in the novel before "they came" reappears later and has a deeply unsettling effect on the reader. One of the major challenges of translating a novel set in Bosnia and Herzegovina, a world relatively foreign to the UK reader, was presenting life in rural Central Bosnia in the 1990s. Indeed, some of the obstacles were simple idiomatic phrases in the Croatian language and concepts in Croatian culture that we take for granted there. Consider something as simple as the characters' footwear. The traditional leather shoes, worn by the older characters such as Spasoje and Grandmother, are called *opanci*. As there is no English equivalent, these had to become simply 'leather shoes'. Translating the footwear of the other characters was trickier. They constantly wear *papuče*, which are, in one word, slippers. However, these characters, particularly the children, wear slippers both inside and outside. As the rural region where the story is set is relatively poor, very few people could afford more than one pair of shoes or trainers, which were usually only worn on special occasions. This means that the word *papuče* also denotes everyday footwear. But as there is no single English word that can convey all these cultural nuances inherent to *papuče*, my translation of the word had to be split: the shoes the characters wore inside became slippers, and their outdoor shoes flip-flops.

Another simple concept which created translation dilemmas was the term *dvorište*. The Croatian term denotes an enclosed area around a property or a home. At first, it seems the equivalent word in British English would be garden. But the term dvorište is more expansive than the British 'garden'. Dvorište also includes the driveway outside the house, which in this case is a dirt track, as well as shelters for livestock – a pie sty, barn or chicken coop – and other buildings necessary for farm life. The cultural implications of a farming lifestyle innate to the word dvorište are not implied by the English 'garden'; instead, the word 'yard' felt closer to dvorište for its connotations of an area out the front of the house, and more suitable for a rural space.

Just these two examples show that even the most common words require thought and research to get across to the reader the world presented by the author. My thanks to Tasja Dorkofikis and Gesche Ipsen for pointing out these discrepancies during the copy-editing stage and for their suggestions to render faithfully the translation of the original text.

- How would you describe your approach to literary translation more generally? Do you think that the translator should be an invisible mediator that renders the target language such that the readers can experience the novel exactly as they can the original work? Or is the act of translation inevitably the writing of a new piece of work, with its own unique intricacies?

Although I subscribe to the translator being an invisible mediator, every translation, be it from one language to another or from Mediaeval English to modern English inevitably becomes an adaptation of the original text. Despite attempts to adhere to the original, there are many elements and phrases that must be altered to be idiomatic in the target language and this inevitably affects the final translation.

The Croatian language, like most Slavic languages, is a highly inflected language – a language in which the form or endings of words are changed to indicate their function in the sentence – and, besides having seven grammatical cases, has a very loose word order. In Croatian, the subject of a sentence does not need to be explicitly expressed as it is clear from the verb form. Because of this, many of Magdalena's sentences are short and clipped. This presented a slight stylistic problem in translation: many of Magdalena's sentences, in the English, would have contained 'there is' or 'there are'. However, as *In Late Summer* is told from the perspective of a young child, so I opted to translate them as sentence fragments.

- What, if anything, would you like readers of *In Late Summer* to take away from their reading experience?

I hope that I have been able to faithfully render the pathos of war told from the perspective of a child who was an innocent victim. The novel also brings home the reality of war: everyone is a victim and repercussions are still felt on both a personal and social level long after the peace agreement has been signed and decades have passed. War leaves nobody indifferent or unscathed. This is masterfully depicted in Magdalena's poignant tale of a little girl who dreamt of growing up and moving to a city yet never got the chance because "they came," bringing Death with them.

Founded in 2023, Linden Editions is dedicated to publishing outstanding literary works of fiction, narrative non-fiction, reportage and essays. These are primarily in translation, from Europe, the Francophonie and the Mediterranean region.

We live and work internationally and enjoy a mixture of cultures, identities and traditions. We intend to use this access to world literature to discover books that merit international exposure: books which tell compelling stories; books which bring fresh, unforgettable voices; and books which are committed, urgent and challenging.

Linden trees grow all over the world, and are often planted at the centre of village squares. People have been gathering under their shade for generations to share stories. Many cultures see the linden tree as sacred, its perfume all-pervading, and its tea curative. Just like the seeds spread by linden trees, we hope our books will spread the seeds of internationalism further.

To discover more, visit lindeneditions.com.

LINDEN TITLES PUBLISHED AND OUT SOON

Voracious · Małgorzata Lebda
translated from the Polish by Antonia Lloyd-Jones

In Late Summer · Magdalena Blažević
translated from the Croatian by Anđelka Raguž

Struck · Susanna Bissoli
translated from the Italian by Georgia Wall

Not There · Mariusz Szczygieł
translated from the Polish by Antonia Lloyd-Jones

Milk and Blood · Agnès de Clairville
translated from the French by Frank Wynne

My Deformed Body · Egana Djabbarova
translated from the Russian by Lisa C. Hayden